"Will That Be All?" She Asked.

She stared at him for a moment, daring him to look back up at her. Did she imagine it, or did his fingers tighten around the pen? He paused in his reading, tugged at his collar, then glanced at her.

"Yes, Sara." He said her name slowly, emphatically, his dark eyes unblinking. Her stomach flipped and she held herself steady.

His full lips straightened into a hard line.

Lips that had kissed her with force and tenderness she could never have imagined. Lips that had teased and tempted her into a frenzy of passion.

Lips that held the power to fire her, as she'd invited him to do on her first day.

Yes, she'd failed once.

She wanted him to know it would *never* happen again.

P9-APJ-160

Dear Reader,

Telling your boss you're pregnant is always hard, but what if it's his baby? I remember agonizing over when to tell my boss I was pregnant, and this was a female boss not even slightly implicated in the conception. We all know that having a baby changes *everything*.

I never did go back to that job after my maternity leave, and I can credit one of my babies with helping me get serious about writing. My daughter woke up at four a.m., ready for action, every morning for her first two years. (Yes, that's TWO YEARS). When she finally started sleeping through until seven-thirty, guess who was still waking up at four?

So there I was with all those empty hours of blissful peace and quiet to sit at the computer and make up stories. Even though my daughter is now in kindergarten, I still get up in the dark to enjoy those magical hours hanging out with my characters before the day begins.

I hope you enjoy Sara and Elan's story!

Jennifer

JENNIFER LEWIS

THE BOSS'S DEMAND

Silhouette® Desire

Published by Silhouette Books

America's Publisher of Contemporary Romance

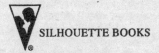

SILHOUETTE BOOKS

ISBN-13: 978-0-373-76812-7
ISBN-10:   0-373-76812-5

THE BOSS'S DEMAND

Copyright © 2007 by Jennifer Lewis

Books by Jennifer Lewis

Silhouette Desire

The Boss's Demand #1812

JENNIFER LEWIS

has been dreaming up stories for as long as she can remember and is thrilled to be able to share them with readers. She has lived on both sides of the Atlantic and worked in media and the arts before she grew bold enough to put pen to paper. She is happily settled in New York with her family, and she would love to hear from readers at jen@jen-lewis.com.

For Michael, Jordan and Mia,
my favorite people in the world.

Acknowledgments:

Thanks to all the people who read this book at various
stages, including Amanda, Anne, Barb, Betty, Car, Cece,
Cheryel, Kathy, Joanne, Leeanne, Marie and Mish.
Special thanks to Carol and Kelle for your insight into
aspects of the oil industry.

One

"I want her gone."

Elan Al Mansur's low-pitched command shot into her ear as she pressed the intercom button to speak with him. Surprise made Sara catch her breath—he must have someone in his office. She held her tongue, afraid of her new boss though she'd only been there a few hours.

"But Mr. Al Mansur…" Sara recognized the voice of Jill Took from Human Resources. "She has a bachelor's degree in business with a minor in geology, she wrote her honors thesis on the profit potential of alternative mining technologies, and her references are excellent."

They were talking about her.

Her finger quivered on the button as her brain told her to hang up. But she stifled her breathing and kept her finger in place.

"Did I not inform you that I require my assistant to be a *mature* woman?" His voice was almost a growl.

"Yes, but…"

"How old is Miss Daly?"

"Twenty-five, but she seems exceptionally mature. She presented herself…"

"Twenty-five!" Sara heard a dismissive snort. "That's hardly what I would call mature. I've made it quite clear that I prefer my assistant to be a woman with decades of experience, and preferably gray hairs on her head."

Sara's finger twitched on the button as her hackles rose. She took in a measured gulp of air.

"Mr. Al Mansur, I'm afraid we don't receive many applications from senior citizens. I…"

"Is Miss Daly married?"

"No, sir, I don't believe she is. But as you know, sir, that kind of information is not—"

Jill paused and Sara pressed the phone to her ear as she heard a loud creak and some rustling. Elan Al Mansur must have silenced Jill with a gesture.

"Miss Took—" His throaty voice coiled into Sara's ear and fear curled in her stomach at his tone. "I'm a busy man. I don't have time for the whims and fancies of foolish girls. We both know the kinds of problems which have plagued my office of late. Miss Daly must go."

"But Mr. Al Mansur…"

"That's my last word on the matter. *Miss Daly?*"

Sara jumped in her chair as her name assaulted her down the phone line. He must have pressed the intercom button, too.

"Yes," she croaked.

"Please, come in."

"Yes, sir." She hung up the phone gingerly. Adrenaline spiked through her body. *I'm going to be fired.*

She could hear the murmur of their voices on the other side of the heavy mahogany door, no doubt discussing the terms of her severance. Her severance? After one morning? She'd moved a thousand miles from her home in Wisconsin to take this job in Placer, amidst the crumpled peaks and wide valleys of Nevada's high desert. All her cash had gone into the security deposit on her apartment and her car had died and... The horror of the situation bloomed like a thunderhead.

This job was the answer to all her prayers. The high salary was her ticket out from under the crushing load of debt from her college loans and her mother's final illness. It had taken her extra time to get her degree while holding down a full-time job, and finally here was an opportunity to build her career and make her reputation as Executive Assistant and Project Manager at one of the fastest growing players in the oil industry.

Now it would be taken from her because she didn't have any gray in her hair?

It wasn't fair. To work so hard for so long and not even be given a chance to prove herself? *No. Not today, Mr. Al Mansur.* She didn't plan to leave quietly.

Fear and rage fought inside her as she rose from her chair. Buttoning the jacket of the conservative suit she'd bought especially for the job, she strode toward the door. Her hand trembled as she reached for the large brushed-steel handle, and she inhaled sharply as she pressed down the lever.

"But she's a plain little thing, I'm sure she wouldn't be the type to..." Ms. Took's words trailed off and pink flushed her cheeks as Sara made her entrance.

Her boss's focused black gaze hit her like a right hook to the gut. He leaned back in a black leather chair, arms on the armrests, surveying her down the length of his aristocratic nose.

Everything about the man seemed designed to intimidate. From his thick black hair and hard-edged features to his broad muscled frame in its tailored black suit, Elan Al Mansur seethed with power and danger.

Sara's angry protest withered on her tongue as he leaned forward in his chair, narrowed his eyes, and pursed his lips slightly.

"Miss Daly."

"Yes." She was surprised her voice sounded so normal as she gagged on a ferocious cocktail of terror and indignation.

His gaze drifted over her face, disdain plain in his raised eyebrow and slightly curled lip.

Anger simmered inside Sara along with an unfamiliar sensation. An odd tension that tightened her muscles and nerves, wound them taut like the strings of an instrument as a searing note of high-pitched anxiety rose in the air.

His eyes locked on hers. "You're being reassigned to a position in accounting. Your salary and benefits will remain the same. You'll begin your duties immediately."

Accounting? She'd moved here to take a highly visible position as right hand to the CEO, with assurances that her duties would range far beyond administrative tasks. A transfer to accounting was a step backward. A slap in the face.

"But why?" The words shot out before she had a chance to shape them into an intelligent question.

Jill Took shifted awkwardly in her chair, "Er, we believe your skill set and attention to detail will be better employed in, er, other capacities."

Sara tore her eyes from Miss Took and fixed them back on the man who wanted her gone. He didn't even know her and already he despised her.

Instead of shrinking in the face of his distaste, she felt her assertive impulse growing, swelling, threatening to burst its boundaries.

But she had everything to lose and nothing to gain from alienating this man. *Proceed with caution.*

His arrogant features had an unsettling beauty to them. Some women might find him attractive. But to her he was simply a boss.

An ordinary man in a dark suit who just happened to have eyes that tore through flesh and bone with the intensity of their gaze.

She stared at him for a full five seconds and he didn't flinch. A curious expression lit his unblinking eyes. His lips parted slightly but he didn't speak. At last, he leaned forward—his chair let out a violent creak—and reached for a pen on his desk.

"You'll be compensated for your inconvenience, Miss Daly."

"I don't want compensation." At last her repressed ire bubbled over into speech. "I want this job. I'm qualified for this job and I'm a hard worker. I'll be the best assistant you've ever had, I promise you that, Mr. Al Mansur. You will find no fault with me."

She could hardly believe she was begging to keep a job with a man who obviously didn't want her around, but she was damned if she'd let a career opportunity of this magnitude be snatched rudely away.

"That will not be possible, Miss Daly."

His poker face and easy posture threw fresh fuel on the flames of her indignation.

"I overheard your conversation." The words slipped out before she had time to consider the consequences. Good. It was time to lay all her cards on the table.

He raised an eyebrow and a shadow clouded his face. He blinked once, then his fierce eyes tunneled into her again with harrowing intensity.

Sara struggled for breath, for strength to defend herself. "I heard you say I'm not old enough for the position."

"Er, Miss Daly—" Jill Took rose from her chair, but ceased speaking when her boss raised his hand.

"Miss Daly, I'll be frank with you." His voice was deep, his tone casual. He leaned back in his chair—creak!—and crossed his arms over his chest. Sara couldn't help noticing how thick his upper arms were, even through the wool of his suit.

"I've had my fill of flighty girls who are here merely to hunt for a husband. Don't think I flatter myself that I'm the object of their attentions. Frankly, I find them pathetic."

He looked down his slightly aquiline nose at her for a second and the full force of his disgust threatened to knock her off her feet.

"I have a business to run and I will no longer tolerate the foolish behavior of those who have anything other than my business on their mind. For this reason I shall no longer consider young, single women for this position."

He leaned forward again—creak!—and picked up a pen off the desk. As if to sign her death warrant. "That will be all, Miss Daly."

A rush of exasperation propelled Sara to his desk. She placed her fingertips on the polished mahogany and leaned toward him. Close enough to taste his scent—subtle and masculine—the fragrance of a deodorant soap released by warm, active skin.

He leaned back slowly, surveying her, arms crossed over his chest. Listening.

Now she was on the offensive.

"Mr. Al Mansur, I may be a young, single woman, but, believe me, I have no interests beyond performing this job to the best of my abilities. I am an experienced executive assistant."

And a plain little thing. Plain, was she? So much the better. She lifted her chin and fixed her gaze directly on his dark eyes. He narrowed them slightly.

She sucked in a breath. "Your company is the kind of fast-growing, forward-thinking firm I want to work for. You've achieved revenue growth of ten percent a year over the last five years. You're a leader in exploiting new drilling technologies and reducing environmentally harmful emissions at your drilling sites."

She steadied herself, refused to wilt in the heat of his scorching stare. "Your company has won praise for creating a progressive labor-friendly work environment. Praise it may not deserve, given the way I'm being treated. And if you take this job away from me I'll *sue* you for reverse age discrimination."

As her words reverberated off the stark white walls of his office, she sprang back from the desk. She crossed her arms over her chest, mirrored his defensive gesture. Her assertiveness thrilled her—and appalled her. A lawsuit? She couldn't even afford a two-piece suit. She was bluffing, but what the heck, she didn't have much to lose.

Well, except the position in accounting. Which did still have the same excellent salary and benefits. Recrimination snaked in her gut. She was playing pretty high-stakes poker with her life right now.

His face tightened as he watched her. His black eyes burned with intensity that sent an icy shiver up her spine. If looks could kill… Perhaps looks *could* kill? The one he gave her right now seemed to be sapping her life force in an alarming way.

On second thought, Mr. Al Mansur, perhaps counting a few beans…

"You…" He uttered the single word in a voice so deep it was barely within the human range of hearing.

He paused, then rose from his chair in a single swift motion.

"You…" Rage crackled in his throaty speech and sparked in his eyes. He rested a big hand on the desk, amidst the piles of papers and stacks of files that covered its surface. Awareness of his threatening physique cowed her as he leaned across the desk, a muscle working in his jaw. "*You*—will sue *me?*"

"It's not fair. You haven't given me a chance. You're firing me for something someone else has done." She sounded calm and rational, though she felt anything but. "Let me prove to you I can do this job. If you aren't happy with my performance, then you can transfer me or fire me outright and I won't complain."

He considered her for a moment, brow furrowed. Then he drew himself up and crossed his arms over his chest. He shot a glance at Jill Took, then looked back at Sara with one eyebrow raised.

"All right, Miss Daly. You shall have one month."

She sagged with glorious relief.

"One month to prove that you can keep your mind focused on your duties."

"You won't be disappointed, sir." She resisted the urge to add a military salute.

Her shoulders locked with sudden anxiety as he strode around his desk. Disobeying the instinct to shrink from his approach, she forced herself to stand steady. She took his offered hand and shook it with what she hoped was authoritative firmness. Big and warm, his hand gripped hers for a mere instant.

And in that instant she realized the magnitude of the challenge before her.

An invisible shudder rocked her as his skin touched hers. His dark eyes seemed to see right through her, their piercing gaze penetrating to the core of her being. Everything in her pricked up—ears, hair, goose bumps—agonizingly aware of the danger-ously male life force before her.

When she drew her hand back it tingled slightly. Her body flushed with sudden heat that belied the air-conditioned chill of the office. If not for the stiff fabric of her new suit, her newly tightened nipples would be clearly visible.

What on earth?

Chemistry? Sara stepped backward, blinking, afraid of the strange sensations surging through her. How could a man she didn't know—a man she didn't like at all—have this kind of effect on her?

Oh, dear.

She cleared her throat, desperate to get control of her errant body and mind and demonstrate the focused professionalism she'd promised.

"Will that be all, sir?" She sounded like a movie character. Right now she needed a script.

She needed to get out of there.

ASAP.

Her boss had turned away to rifle through the mess of papers sprawled over his huge desk.

"Hmph," he grunted, without looking up. Then he nodded dismissively to the two women. "Thank you."

Jill Took rose from her chair and bolted for the door. Sara scurried behind her like a startled rabbit.

Outside in the spacious annex that held Sara's desk, Jill turned to her.

"Sara, what I was saying when you came in, about you being a plain little thing…" Her cheeks turned pink again. "You know I was just trying anything I could think of to get Mr. Al Mansur to change his mind."

"Of course." Sara nodded vigorously, wondering why Jill's cheeks were so pink if she wasn't fibbing. "And I appreciate you standing up for me. I won't let you down."

"I know you won't. I hired you, remember?"

Sara laughed a little, glad to release some tension.

Jill lowered her voice. "He's all right really. It's just that, well, he's right, quite honestly. I hired his last two assistants. They appeared to be perfectly capable, suitable employees, very polished and efficient, but they… I don't know how to explain it. They went gaga over him." Jill widened her eyes comically.

Sara blinked and swallowed. She'd tasted a sip of gaga and was still tipsy from it.

"I mean, he's a good-looking guy and all," Jill continued quietly, with a quick glance at the closed door. "But he has some kind of bizarre effect on women that makes them throw themselves at him in the most embarrassing way. I could tell you weren't that sort at all."

Since you're such a plain little thing.

The unspoken words hung in the air between them. Sara shrank like Alice in Wonderland before the immaculately attired thirty-something blonde in her designer suit and high heels. Apparently Jill was impervious to whatever strange curse of irresistibility hung over the head of poor Elan. Sara felt thoroughly humbled.

"Not at all," she managed. "I need this job and I mean to keep it."

"You'll do great," Jill said, giving her a reassuring squeeze on the arm.

Sara nodded resolutely. "You bet I will."

Sue him for reverse age discrimination, would she? Elan raised his eyebrows. That was a first. She obviously knew little about discrimination law, but it stung that she'd thought to accuse him of bias.

He had nothing against female employees. He'd even hire them out in the oil fields if they wanted the work.

But he wanted nothing more to do with simpering maidens who draped themselves across his desk and fluttered their eyelashes over his morning coffee. They exhausted him with their intrigues and flirtations. And none of them could even make a decent cup of coffee. Weak—the coffee and the women.

He looked up at a knock on the door. "Come in."

Sara entered with a report he'd asked her to prepare and placed the file on his desk.

"Can I get you anything?" Her voice rang in his silent office like a bell. She waited quietly. A strand of pale hair had come loose from her bun and fluttered near her chin, which lifted in a gesture of defiance.

"I could use a cup of coffee." He cocked his head.

"I don't know how to make coffee." She stared at him, her attitude almost insolent. He leaned forward in his chair, struck by her refusal.

"I suspect you have the aptitude to figure it out," he said slowly. "But never mind. Too much caffeine rattles the nerves."

He saw a slight smile tug at the corners of her mouth, but she quickly gained control of her features and regarded him once again with a stony expression.

He'd felt the sharp edge of her attitude and he had to admit he liked it. She stood her ground admirably.

She leaned over to replace the cap on a pen lying open on his desk. The loose strand of hair hung momentarily in her eyes and she raised a hand to brush it aside. As she tucked the lock behind her ear she looked up at him, caught off guard, and their eyes met.

A mute challenge.

Suddenly his office seemed uncomfortably warm.

She turned and left without another word. A good sign. She wouldn't bend his ear with idle chitchat.

He'd give her the chance she asked for. That she'd demanded. He'd seen the fire that flared in her eyes. Eyes the color of rare jade, cool and flecked with gold. Fringed with pale lashes that had blinked in anger as she'd stared him down.

A plain little thing? What an expression. He was amused by the way some people defined beauty in terms of how loudly it shouted at you. For him, true beauty was a quality that shone from within, that brightened and strengthened, like the morning sun rising behind dark mountains. A force that could be dangerous to its beholder.

But Sara's quiet beauty had no effect on him. He'd grown used to enjoying the more obvious kind of feminine attributes. When in Rome... Fast cars, fast women and the comfort and ease of being alone in his bed at the end of the day.

No ties, no responsibilities, no commitments. Something that would be unheard of, horrifying even, to the people he'd left behind in Oman.

But he had everything he needed here, including freedom from the crippling bonds of traditions that had no place in the modern world.

* * *

Sara spent much of the afternoon rearranging the files in her desk. Her predecessor's organizational system baffled her. But then it didn't sound like she'd been there long. Nor had the woman before her or the one before that.

Had they all fallen victim to the dangerous charms of a boss who wanted nothing more than an efficient worker?

She smoothed the last of her newly printed labels on her neatly rearranged file folders and eased the drawer shut.

Her boss emerged from his office and walked past her desk without saying a word or even looking in her direction. He strode across the floor with the powerful gait of a predator.

As the tall mahogany door to the elevator lobby closed behind him, Sara reflected that Elan himself must be the reason this job came with hardship pay. She could already see he worked like a demon and expected his employees to do the same.

Oh, she could be a demon all right.

She felt a little circumspect about entering his office when he was away, but he hadn't actually told her to keep out. She planned to organize it in a such a way that he'd wonder how he ever survived without her.

She pushed open the door and stepped into the hushed space. No paintings or statues, not a single photograph ornamented his desk. Elan was clearly all business all the time.

She'd felt it necessary to establish that she was not the coffee waitress, but now she was keen to prove she'd do everything in her power to make Elan's day run smoothly. With brisk efficiency, she sorted and rearranged the disarray of papers on his desk, labeling them with sticky notes if they required action. She sharpened his pencils and tested his pens, threw away any dry ones.

She'd rustled up a can of WD-40 to rid his chair of its infuriating squeak. Proud to be a roll-up-the-sleeves type of person, she was on her hands and knees under the chair when the door opened.

"What on earth…?" Her boss's deep voice rumbled across the silent office. From her vantage point under the desk she could see two shiny black brogues, and the crisp cuffs of his pinstriped suit.

A fist of apprehension seized her gut and she obeyed the instinctive urge to leap to her feet.

"Ouch!" She banged her head hard on the underside of the chair.

The brogues took a step forward and Sara swallowed hard. She maneuvered out from under the massive chair and clambered to her feet with as much dignity as her fitted skirt would allow.

The sunset streaming through the wall of windows made her blink. As did the sight of Elan, his broad shoulders silhouetted in the doorway. His suit jacket was unbuttoned and his tie loosened, revealing a glimpse of dark throat that beckoned her eyes.

The harsh features of his face gleamed like rare metal in the copper rays of the lowering sun as he stared at her, dark brows lowered over narrowed eyes.

He looked down at the shining mahogany surface that had previously been covered by papers, then at her, and the can in her hand.

"What are you doing?"

She cleared her throat. "Your chair creaks."

One black brow raised.

"Didn't you notice? It's been driving me crazy. Let's see if I got it." She jumped down into the seat of the enormous leather chair and was pleased to hear absolutely nothing. "I think I nailed it."

He hadn't moved a muscle. "What have you done to my desk?" He wrenched his eyes from hers to the newly uncluttered expanse of mahogany.

"I sorted your papers into relevant categories. I didn't throw anything away, but the pile on the left can go, I think."

He frowned at her. His face darkened and suspicion clouded his eyes. "How could you possibly know enough about my work to organize my papers on your first day?"

"Instinct."

But all instinct fled as her skin began to sizzle under Elan's searing gaze.

"Please rise from my chair." He spoke slowly, as if attempting to communicate with someone with a poor command of the language.

She jolted to her feet. She'd been so transfixed by him she'd forgotten she was lounging in his personal throne.

His dark pupils tracked her with laser-beam intensity. "What made you think you could enter my office and handle my effects without permission?"

She struggled to regain her professional demeanor. "I consider keeping your desk organized to be one of my responsibilities."

He lowered his head slightly, scrutinizing her. "How do I know you weren't placing a bug there?"

"A bug?"

"To record my conversations."

Indignation stung her. "Are you saying anything worth recording?"

She immediately regretted her childish pique.

Elan stared at her. His brow furrowed as he digested her insolence. But his reply was measured, calm.

"To my business rivals, yes." He strode across the room and maneuvered around her. He quickly crouched down and reached a hand under the seat of the chair.

Sara found her eyes resting on his neck, on the strip of tan skin between the starched collar of his white shirt and the close-cropped black hair at the base of his skull. His small, delicate ear was at odds with the massive, powerful build of his body.

He knelt on the floor and reached an arm under his desk. The roping muscles of his back, visible even though the dark fabric of his suit, captured her attention. It took a few seconds before she realized he was feeling the underside of the desk, searching for electronic devices.

Anger at his suspicion pricked her. She'd never been accused of criminal activity before, and distrust didn't sit well with her. She'd worked at one job or another since age fourteen, and the admiration and satisfaction of her boss had always been something she could count on.

Elan leaned further under the desk. His suit jacket lifted, revealing the curve of his rear. Good Lord, the man was built like a decathlete.

She took a step backward, trying to regain control as a sudden swell of heat made her body uncomfortable inside the stiff fabric of her suit.

He backed slowly out from under the desk while she tried to look anywhere except at his well-muscled backside. Elan avoided looking at her, too, as he pulled himself awkwardly back up to his feet.

"Still think I'm a mole?" She cocked her head, daring him to extend his accusation.

He ran a hand through his thick hair. "Your previous job was with an electronics firm, no?"

"Yes, Bates Electronics. I worked there for two years. They have no relationship to the oil industry that I know of and no reason to engage in industrial espionage. I am not a spy."

"Couldn't you have alerted building maintenance to the fact that my chair creaks?"

"Sure, but by the time I'd called them, explained the problem and demonstrated the squeak, I could have fixed it myself. There's nothing highly specialized about spraying lubricant."

He looked at her. The word *lubricant* hung in the air between them. An innocent word, related to the greasing of cogs, the oiling of hinges, the wetting of pistons. Images which sent Sara's mind spinning in all sorts of forbidden directions.

She remembered his warnings against showing any prurient interest in him. The thought triggered a rash impulse to test

Elan's sense of humor by asking if she could be fired for saying the word *lubricant* in his presence.

Mercifully she held her tongue. She dug her fingernails into her palms, tried to control the craziness goading her. Why on earth would she want to provoke and irritate her new boss?

She had an almost irresistible urge to see what lay behind the highly polished granite facade Elan Al Mansur presented to the world.

He drew himself up, took off his suit jacket and hung it over the back of his chair. Unhooked his gold cuff links, dropped them on the desk and rolled up his sleeves. His forearms were muscled, brown and dusted with black hair.

The thought of those forearms closing around her waist, holding her tight, swept through her mind like a gale-force wind.

She stepped backward and smoothed the front of her suit with a hand, trying to brush away the bizarre physical sensation assailing her.

Elan pushed his shirtsleeves up above his elbows as he settled into his chair. Sara suspected her face was blazing as she struggled to keep her eyes off his arms. An arm, for crying out loud! What on earth was wrong with her?

The watch on that arm probably cost more than her mother's last round of chemo treatments. It was gold, the white face covered with dials. Probably a Rolex. She suspected nothing but the best was good enough for Elan Al Mansur.

"You have no work to do, Sara?" He looked up from his papers, fixing her with a slit-eyed stare. She jumped inwardly.

"I wasn't sure if you needed anything."

"If I want something, I'll let you know." One broad finger rested on the page, marking his place. "In the meantime, I'll expect you to provide your own entertainment."

He'd been aware of her eyes on him, studying him, appraising him. Enjoying him. Humiliation clenched her gut. She turned swiftly away as she felt a renewed blush darken her cheeks.

"Would you like me to change the water in that vase of roses?" From one of his legions of tormented admirers, no doubt.

He looked at her for a moment.

"No." He glanced back to his papers. "Perhaps you could take them home? I don't like flowers."

"I can't take them home, I ride a bike to work. But I'll put them on my desk. They'll brighten the place up a bit. Thanks."

She paused to bury her face in the yellow blooms. The soothing scent of rose petals filled her senses, relaxed her.

"They're lovely."

"Not to me. They'll be dead in a day or two. I don't wish to watch them die."

"I'll enjoy their swan song. If you don't need anything else, I'll take off for the day."

He glanced quickly at his expensive watch. "Fine." He went back to shuffling a concertina of papers between his powerful fingers. She lifted the vase and moved toward the door, opened it with her hip.

"Good night." She turned to him.

Lowered in concentration, his face was hidden from her until he raised it. "You ride a bike to work?"

"Yes." She paused, waiting for his disapproval.

"I see." He looked at her for a moment, stony features unreadable. Then he turned back to his papers, opened his pen, and etched a dramatic signature into the crisp white document on his desk.

Sara slipped out through the door with a silent sigh of relief and heard it close softly behind her.

Elan placed the signed papers in his out-box and rose slowly from his chair. He stood in front of the floor-to-ceiling window that looked over the parking lot toward the desert and the distant mountain range beyond.

The sun hung low in the sky, glinting off geometric rows of cars baking in the late-afternoon sun. Many employees had already left. The rest were striding across the parking lot, climbing into their cars and driving out through the gates in an orderly fashion like so many instinctive ants.

A lone figure broke from the orderly procession of cars, darting among them, zigzagging across the parking lot on a bicycle.

Sara.

He narrowed his eyes, straining to get a better look at her. She'd changed out of her beige suit. Of course, who would ride a bicycle in a tight skirt? Well, not tight, but fitted, hugging the curve of her hips gently, as he recalled rather too clearly.

She'd put on shorts. Bicycle shorts, the stretchy kind. He blinked. Swallowed. Her legs were lean, muscled, powerful. Her tawny hair was tied back in a ponytail. Shouldn't she be wearing a helmet?

He tracked her movements across the parking lot as she made a diagonal path to the exit while the long line of cars wound patiently around the edge of the lot. She stood on her pedals as she went over a speed bump, lifted her backside into the air.

He coughed and turned away. Experienced a sudden rush of uncomfortable sensation. Something stirred inside him that surprised and annoyed him. His pulse pounded and he opened his mouth to breathe.

He moved away from the window and undid another button on his shirt to loosen it. The powerful visual of Sara's raised hips taunted him.

A plain little thing? Not so. She merely plied her feminine charms in a more calculated fashion than the girls in miniskirts and high heels.

But already he could see she was no different from the others.

Two

"You may call me Elan."

The rumble of his voice echoed in a previously undiscovered part of her anatomy. She swallowed hard.

"All right, Elan."

His name, spoken in her voice, sounded strangely intimate. The intimacy was a gift to cherish, a reward for her successful first week on the job. She knew he was pleased with her performance. Twice he'd sent her to meetings in his place, and he'd even allowed her to negotiate a new contract with a pipe supplier.

She'd hoped the allure of his masculine charms would fade with time and overexposure. That, unfortunately, had not yet happened.

"Sara, here's my speech for the conference next week. Please proof it and give me your opinion."

He lifted a sheaf of handwritten papers. She noted with chagrin that even his writing was sexy. Bold, thick cursive flowed black from his solid-gold fountain pen.

"I'd be glad to." She took the papers and forced herself not to linger on the seductive thickness of his muscled neck as he bent his head to the stack of contracts she'd handed him.

Elan threw himself into his job with the intensity of a competitive athlete. At the end of the day he looked so tense that she longed to move behind his chair and massage the hard ridges of his shoulders. Longed to hear him sigh with relief as her fingers eased the knots beneath his skin, soothing his tension. Longed to lose her fingertips in the snowy cotton of his shirt, the thick darkness of his hair.

She fought these urges like the beckoning calls to madness they were. A foolish schoolgirl crush that undermined her competence. No possible good could come from sighing over a man who'd made it clear he despised the attentions of female employees. This was the man who held the key to her future in his hands.

Broad, capable hands that haunted her imagination.

"You can read my speech in here if you wish. You won't be disturbed by your ringing phone." He indicated a plum-colored leather chair tucked in a corner of his vast office.

"Great, thanks." Another honor she probably didn't deserve. She settled herself in the soft leather and propped the papers up in front of her eyes, the better to block out any distracting view of her boss.

The more they worked together, the more she was bedeviled by the urge to touch him. Electricity crackled in the air when she came within inches of him, which was often as she worked closely with him throughout the day. But the tiny distance between them was an unbridgeable chasm whose howling depths threatened to engulf her if she were foolish enough to act.

Perhaps a little touch would be enough, a casual brush of the hand.

She couldn't jump off that cliff. This job was too important. And not just for the badly needed money it provided; Elan was giving her a chance to prove herself in the business world, to build a career that would be the foundation for a secure life.

With a successful career she'd never be stuck depending on a man to support her. She'd never have to suffer the way her mother had, trapped in a loveless marriage because she had too many hungry mouths to feed.

But something about the ridge of Elan's cheekbone made her long to bite it gently. Something about his ear called her to trace its delicate curve with a soft fingertip and suck the tender, unpierced lobe. Something about his mouth made her want to part his unsmiling lips with her tongue and plunge into the warm depths.

"What are you looking at?"

She jumped in her seat, totally busted as Elan stared at her, one eyebrow slightly lifted. She blinked, eyelids darting over her lust-dilated pupils. He'd seen her gawking at him over the top of his speech, desire written all over her face.

"I'm sorry, just thinking."

"I can see that." He settled back against the black leather of his chair. His eyes narrowed slightly and the barest shadow of a smile played over his lips.

He knew she wanted him. Just like all those other women had wanted him. She struggled to hold his black gaze, trying not to flinch as he stared, unblinking, taunting her with her own unspoken desires.

He raised one hand, extended a single long finger and brought it slowly to his lips. A thoughtful, deliberate, unbearably sensual gesture. A surge of warmth heated Sara's body, pleasurable and uncomfortable at the same time.

Her suit felt tight, constricting, holding in a body that longed to break free, to give rein to all the crazy impulses jarring her nerves and sending suggestions to her muscles that made her strain to hold her limbs still.

A knock on the door startled her, and she leaped to her feet, dropping Elan's speech unceremoniously in the chair.

"You're jumpy," he murmured.

"Come in," she said sharply, trying to regain the air of prim efficiency she used to pride herself on.

"I've got the samples you requested from the Davis field." Dora entered, her coral mouth pursed in a polite smile. The office gossip, she took far too much pleasure in regaling Sara with tales of her predecessors' downfall.

Dora carried a rectangular metal basket filled with vials of a black substance.

"I'll take them." Sara, lifted the heavy basket by its handles. She looked at Elan for instructions.

"On the desk."

She lowered the basket and put it right on top of the scattered papers as he'd indicated. He picked up one of the vials.

"Thank you, Dora." Elan dismissed her with a nod. She exited with a slight smirk on her face that made Sara's insides twist with affront. Could Dora see into her mind? Know she was tempted down the same path to self-destruction that had tripped up so many women before her?

"Do you know what this is?" He swirled it and the dark liquid clung to the sides of the glass, viscous, slightly metallic.

"Oil?"

"Yes. The reason we're all here." He watched the liquid settle back down into the bottom of the vial. "Black gold."

He removed the lid and lifted the vial to his nostrils. He held it under his nose for a moment, then let out a little grunt of satisfaction. "I never grow tired of this smell." He rose and moved around the desk toward her. "Have you ever handled crude oil?"

"Can't say I have," said Sara. Awareness of his physical presence made her palms tingle.

Elan dipped one of his long fingers into the neck of the jar, plunged it into the thin, black liquid and withdrew it. "Here." He extended his finger under her nose, invited her to sample its bouquet. She wrinkled her nose and suppressed a sudden urge to laugh. The strong crude-oil smell assaulted her senses, a little intoxicating.

Elan lifted his finger to his own nose. On errant impulse, she reached up and pushed his finger gently, so the oil smudged on his upper lip. She'd touched him! She drew her hand back, horrified, her finger quivering. He looked at her in astonishment.

A roiling mass of emotions bubbled up into laughter. "You look like Charlie Chaplin."

His eyes narrowed as he studied her face, and her stomach tightened.

"Perhaps I'm his famous character, the Great Dictator?"

A glint of humor sparked in his eyes and his mouth threatened to curve into a smile. The idea of Elan smiling caused a strange sensation deep in her belly, and she groped mentally for a quick comeback.

"You're a benevolent dictator." She gave him a mocking salute and, slowly, a grin lit his face like the sun bursting out above the horizon.

"I consider that a compliment." The sensual curve of his lips revealed rows of perfectly straight white teeth. His eyes twinkled with amusement as he studied her. The warmth of his smile and the intensity of his gaze combined to seriously undermine her sanity.

"Let me get a tissue for you."

She retrieved one from the box on his desk and raised it to wipe the black smudge from his upper lip. Her fingertips brushed against the skin of his cheek—not rough, yet not soft, either— as she pressed the tissue to his mouth. For a moment she thought she might close her eyes in shameful bliss at finally fulfilling her fantasies of touching Elan.

She bit her lip hard, tried to distract herself from the unsettling physical sensations coursing through her body.

He watched her curiously as she wiped the oil from his lip. It didn't come off particularly easily and she managed to accidentally smudge more of it on his cheek with the dirty tissue.

"Hold on, let me get another." Her heart pounded as she got to touch him again, cleaning the last trace from the crease of his smile.

Deliberate throat-clearing drew their attention as Dora reentered with a second tray of samples. Her face twisted into an expression of amusement concealed with considerable effort. Sara realized it might well look as if she was wiping her own lipstick from the lips and cheek of her boss.

What a thought.

She shoved the oily tissue into her pocket and snatched the second tray of samples. She half expected Elan to make it brusquely clear that nothing had happened. Nothing *had* happened. But he stood, languid in the center of the room, challenging his employee to make what she would of the scene.

Sara made a fuss of rearranging the papers on the desk to make room for the second basket. "Thank you, Dora." The woman nodded and turned for the door, lips primly pressed together.

The door closed behind Dora. Sara turned to Elan and saw a smile glittering in his eyes.

"She believes we were kissing," he said. The throaty rumble of his voice, and the suggestion in his words, made her body tremble slightly. She was perilously close to the edge of the cliff.

"No danger of that," she replied quickly. "Would you like a tissue to clean your finger?"

"Thanks."

She retrieved the tissue, but as she went to hand it to him he merely extended his finger. His gaze met hers and she read a challenge in it.

She wrapped the tissue around his finger, then took hold of his wrist in her other hand to hold it steady. Currents of dangerous energy snaked up her arm from where her fingers circled around his pulse point.

She wiped until his finger was clean, but she was reluctant to let go. Touching Elan was a sweet thrill she wanted to prolong. She dabbed at his skin again as the fingers of her other hand curved under his to support the firm flesh of his palm.

Stop it, Sara! You're playing with fire. Flammable liquids and flammable emotions are not a good combination.

She pulled her hands away and threw the tissues into the wastebasket. Elan remained silent and she sneaked a glance at him. He watched her with an odd expression in his dark eyes.

"I'll read your speech at my desk," she said, gathering the scattered papers. He nodded. She hurried out of the room and closed the door softly behind her, her heart hammering and her mind whirling.

Wanting Elan was taboo. Touching him forbidden. He was unavailable, off-limits. They had a contract, clearly stated. So why was it so easy to imagine his warm breath on her throat, the pressure of his palms on the curve of her waist?

She had a career to build and she wanted to take on more responsibilities. She wanted more influence in the company, and she knew it was hers for the taking.

And she wanted Elan.

The two impulses were opposing, one canceled out the other. To act on her feelings for her boss would be to end her career at this company. That had been made perfectly plain to her on her first day at the job.

She was still on trial.

One week down, three to go.

"What on earth is this?" Elan looked at her, one eyebrow raised in astonishment as he surveyed the expensive new black leather bump on his chair.

"A lumbar support cushion. It helps to keep your back in a comfortable position. I notice you stretch your spine a lot and I thought this might help prevent it getting kinked up in the first place."

Because frankly, I can't watch you stretch and flex like that even one more time and keep the last shreds of my tattered sanity.

He reached out and prodded it with his long, powerful fingers as if it might have a life of its own. "Hmph."

"It's on trial. It goes back if you don't like it. I didn't file the expense report yet." She turned and took the watering can to the row of shiny, dark green plants she'd bought to soften the austere atmosphere of his office.

She hadn't expected him to be thrilled. Surprise and confusion were the emotions she seemed to conjure in Elan with her little extracurricular gestures, though he did a fair job of hiding it.

Maybe she was trying too hard. She'd spent half her Saturday at the gadget store looking at products designed to ease executive stress. She had other ideas for things he might like, but she didn't want to overdo it.

She heard him settle into the leather chair and couldn't resist turning around to catch his reaction. She was annoyed to find herself pathetically hoping to see him smile. He approached the day with grim determination that only tickled her irrational instinct to say or do something totally inappropriate—so she could watch his stony facade crack and catch a glimpse of what lay beneath.

Not so smart. That wasn't what she was here for.

Turned, she saw him sitting uncomfortably in the newly altered chair, brows arched, eyes fixed on her feet.

Uh-oh, no shoes. "Sorry, my shoes were killing me. I'll go put them on."

Elan cleared his throat. "There's no need. It's the end of the day and only you and I are here. You may dress as you wish."

She mentally spanked herself for finding even the most innocent words suggestive when they emerged from Elan's wide, sensual mouth. "Thanks." She forced a polite smile to her lips.

He shifted in the chair as if negotiating a large pea under his mattress.

"You hate it, don't you?"

"I don't hate it, I'm merely unaccustomed to it." He sat up straight and squared his broad shoulders against the chair in a way that made Sara's stomach quiver.

She wrenched her eyes back to the plants and poured water onto the decorative gravel she'd used to cover the soil. The glossy leaves brought life to the room. It was almost cheerful now, especially since she'd convinced him to let her move in a couple of stunning abstract paintings that had languished in a little-used conference room.

"Sara."

Her breath caught—as always—at the sound of her name in his low, husky voice. "Yes?" She continued watering, resisting the urge to turn and look at him.

"It's not your job to water plants in my office, or to make my chair more comfortable." The odd tone of his voice made her look up.

"I know, I just..." She didn't really know exactly what she was doing. Going the extra mile or something.

"Just as I don't expect you to make my coffee, I don't expect you to concern yourself with such trivialities. It's late and you have a home to go to."

She flinched at the stab of pain she felt at his rejection of her efforts. She had only herself to blame. He hadn't asked for any of it.

"I'm sorry. I guess I'm annoying you with all this...stuff." She gestured around the room at the paintings, the plants, the new coffee machine for the viciously strong coffee he brewed. Her heart sank a little. Okay, so she was overdoing it.

"On the contrary. You've made my office very pleasant." He said it quietly, gave her an unexpected, cautious look that squeezed her heart a little.

"To be honest, I enjoy this sort of stuff, you know, cheering things up." She hugged the watering can to her chest. "I have a lot of time on my hands when I'm not here. I'm not used to being on my own. I have a big family back home—four sisters and three brothers." The words tumbled out and the pitch of her voice rose. "My mom was sick for a long time and I took care of her. I'm used to being busy, looking after things, looking after people, you know. I'm not used to going home all alone, I…"

Shut up Sara!

What on earth was she doing running off at the mouth about how pathetically lonely she'd been lately? That wasn't his problem. It had been her decision to move here. To cook for one. To have conversations with herself over the tiny counter in her kitchen. To move the furniture around in her cramped apartment because she had nothing better to do.

To harass her boss with misplaced nurturing instincts. She felt a flush creep above her blouse as she realized what she'd been doing.

His body motionless, Elan spoke softly. "I appreciate the trouble you've taken. It's a gift to understand the needs of others without being asked." He held her gaze, a guarded expression shadowing his hard features. "Your thoughtfulness is a complement to your excellent work."

She blinked and bit her lip as a rush of emotion sprang from something raw inside her. His devastating seriousness and the gravity of such a huge compliment—his first—nearly unhinged her. The urge to cry warred with the urge to explode into raucous laughter.

"Thank you," she managed.

He immediately turned away and began sorting through some papers. Had his dark complexion darkened yet further? She dismissed the thought. He cleared his throat and loosened his necktie with a long finger.

She inhaled a deep breath and accidentally splashed herself with water from the can as she wheeled around to face the door.

"Good night," she muttered as she hustled toward it, feet silent on the carpet.

"Good night, Sara." Low and slightly strangled, as if his tie was still too tight, his words followed her out to her desk, down in the elevator, across the parking lot and home to her silent apartment.

Elan leaned back in his chair and watched as Sara gave a sales pitch to potential clients from Canada. Her trial month was nearly up and she'd proved beyond a shadow of a doubt she was more than worthy of her position.

"As I've demonstrated, our technology is capable of reducing the amount of sediment in the crude oil to well below the required level. The new techniques we have developed allow previously unprofitable fields to be exploited productively. We provide a complete package of services, from drilling to refining, that allow our customers to take advantage of cutting-edge technology and expertise without investing in their own infrastructure."

Her sharp mind and talent for incisive analysis impressed him. They were intriguingly at odds with a soft, warm side of her that caught him off guard with caring gestures. For someone so young she seemed unusually wise, her intelligence matched and even outmeasured by a natural compassion that rather awed him. And those little flashes of humor she surprised him with, well…

The late-afternoon sun shone through the window, glazing her delicate features with gold and sparking fiery highlights in her hair. Her hair looked so soft. He wondered how it would feel between his fingers, under his palms as he cupped her head, tipping it back to claim her mouth in a kiss.

Perish the thought. He would *never* become involved with an employee. Such an action would be an inexcusable abuse of his authority.

He had *never* kissed one of his assistants. Though not through any lack of effort on their part. A woman who would throw herself at a man in a professional environment could *never* command his respect or his affection.

He could not quite understand the appeal he held for them. He did not think his face held such dazzling beauty as to enslave a fellow human. His body was thick and heavy from his work with the horses, not the kind of elegant male form he imagined women would prefer.

Of course there was his wealth. He'd always been wealthy, even before he'd bought a small drilling company coming off a local oil boom and turned it into the thriving oil services corporation it was today. The oil that ran in his blood had enriched his family and his country before he was born. Was this the irresistible appeal he held for women?

No matter. Sara's predecessors had all departed the company of their own free will, rankling under the low opinion he held of them.

But none of them possessed her talent. Already she performed duties far beyond the role she was hired for. Sara was an asset he would hate to lose. And he wouldn't lose her if he could help it.

He'd arranged to have Sara fly with him to the firm's newest drilling site tomorrow. The trip would broaden her understanding of their work and prepare her to take on greater responsibilities.

The object of his thoughts walked across the conference room to the whiteboard and began to sketch out a formula one of the clients had asked to see. His gaze drifted to her hips, to the lush curve of her backside that shifted beneath her suit as she strained to reach the top of the board.

Suddenly his slacks felt a trifle snug. Perhaps he should send his tailor in London some new measurements? He shifted in his chair, tugged at his tie, which now closed too tightly around his neck, constricted his breathing.

Sara dropped her pen. As she bent forward to retrieve it, her skirt strained tightly over the firm length of her thighs and cupped her buttocks. Elan jolted forward in his chair, as a thunderbolt of sensation rammed through him.

He cleared his throat and grabbed hold of his pen, scribbled some meaningless notes on his papers as he struggled to get his errant body back under control.

Her suit was too revealing.

It was indecent and undignified to display so much of one's physique in a business environment. He would have Jill Took from Human Resources address the matter with her.

Slowly he lifted his eyes again as Sara cheerfully explained the calculations involved in an aspect of the refining process. He surveyed the offending suit with an eye to detailed critique, and was chagrined that on closer examination he could not find fault with it. It was not close-fitting. The skirt came well below the knee. It was demure in cut and color.

The problem lay *within* the suit. And within *him*.

Three

"Seventy-six bottles of beer on the wall, seventy-six bottles of beer…" Her voice was cracking, her throat clenched with terror.

"You've survived, Sara, open your eyes." Elan's words penetrated her shattered consciousness.

"Oh, God." Her whole body was rigid. Her eyelids squeezed tight as she struggled to shut out reality.

"We're above the clouds now. There's no danger." His low voice rose over the mellow drone of the jet engines.

Gingerly she opened her eyes, and the bright light gleaming through the row of tiny oval windows threatened to blind her. Silhouetted against it was Elan's face, features creased with concern.

She realized she was clutching both his hands in a death grip. But she couldn't let go. Desire had nothing to do with it. She clung to him out of sheer terror.

"See, it's not so bad. The plane cruises along. You can't even see the ground from up here."

"Oh, God." The thought of the ground miles and miles below made her stomach drop.

"Are you going to be ill?"

Oh, God, please don't let me throw up. "I don't think so."

"Good."

"I'm sorry I'm such a ..." *Wimp? Wuss? Weak woman?*

"Don't apologize, Sara. Many people are afraid of flying." He gave her hands a quick reassuring squeeze.

She took a deep breath, and another. They were airborne. Oh, God.

"You've never flown before?" His look of tender concern caused a swell of emotion to rise to her throat. She swallowed hard.

"No."

"I thought Americans flew everywhere."

"Some do, I guess. Not me." She still couldn't believe they were *above the clouds*. At the thought a fresh surge of horror seized her gut. She saw her anxiety reflected in Elan's pained expression.

He wrenched one of his big hands free from her rigor-mortis clench. As Sara shuddered with—fear?—he unbuckled his seat belt in one swift motion and slid his arm around her shoulder.

The warmth of his sturdy arm encircling her shivering torso soothed her as she leaned into it. She took a deep breath. Maybe she could survive this after all.

"Your family didn't fly abroad on vacation?"

She let out a snort of laughter. A nervous explosion. "No, we rarely left the city limits. My family's finances were strictly hand to mouth."

"They were poor?"

"Very."

"Oh." His lips pursed as he appeared to consider the information. Would it make him think less of her? Surely not. It was hardly her fault. Though she didn't plan to be poor again if she could help it.

"But you're from Wisconsin, aren't you? How did you come to Nevada?"

"By road."

"On your bicycle?" His eyebrows shot up.

She laughed again. The release of laughter and the comfort of his reassuring embrace steadied her nerves.

"No, I drove a car. An old clunker. It died as soon as I got here. That's why I ride a bike now."

He smiled. "I'm relieved to hear it. But you'll buy another car, no?"

"Eventually."

As soon as I pay off tens of thousands of dollars in debt. She didn't really want him to know about that. Her personal burdens were nobody's business.

"The color is returning to your cheeks." He spoke softly. The deep, mellow tone of his voice was intimate, assuring. She gradually became conscious of the way their bodies were entwined. Elan still leaned into her airplane seat, his strength wrapped around her.

His broad chest pushed into her shoulder. The firm surface of his pectorals rubbed against her, heating her through the thin fabric of their clothes. The vibrations from the jet's engine hummed through them both, causing little shock waves of sensation to surge through her, heating and arousing her from head to toe.

The color returned to her cheeks in a blaze of glory.

She tore her eyes from him. As her fear ebbed it was being replaced by an entirely different sensation.

Lust.

His hand rested on her waist just below her right breast. A curl of heat rose in her belly as she became aware of the pad of each long, dexterous finger pushing gently against her skin, warming her through her blouse. Her breast stirred beneath her shirt. Her nipple hardened, craving his touch.

And she was conscious of the scent of him—earthy, musky, with an exotic note of fragrance that wound itself through the air around her.

Elan.

Secret fantasies were coming to life. Dreams stalking the daylight. Her most humiliating craven longing fulfilled in the touch of this man.

Her boss.

As her body tingled with the sensation of sheer physical excitement, her mind struggled with the knowledge that his embrace was purely a gesture of compassion. If he knew what was going on in her body, in her mind, he'd recoil in horror.

But she couldn't help wanting to prolong the illicit pleasure, the dangerous high of being held in the arms of the man whose allure was the torment of her days and the solace of her lonely nights.

Yes, she dreamed about him—waking dreams, as well as sleeping dreams. Fantasies, the shame-laced release of all the pent-up emotion bottled inside her at the end of a long day spent in close proximity to him.

But never as close as this.

On impulse she looked at him and her heart seized as she read the expression in his narrowed eyes.

I want you.

His irises were nearly black, indistinguishable from his pupils, fathomless depths, wells that drew from a dark, secretive soul. But at that moment she knew exactly what was on his mind.

Just as he knew exactly what was on hers.

In a sudden flurry of activity they disentangled themselves. She cleared her throat and smoothed the front of her blouse. He snatched up his *Wall Street Journal* and arranged it in his lap with a good deal of rustling.

He fiddled with his tie. Ran his fingers through his hair.

Unhooked his cuff links and rolled up his sleeves. He shuffled his paper, appearing to scan the columns with keen interest.

Avoiding her glance.

Sara leaned stiffly back into her seat. She had no idea where her briefcase was. In the paralytic terror that had accompanied her onto the aircraft she'd been aware of nothing but an urge to run screaming back down the ramp to the safety of terra firma.

Oddly, though, she wasn't afraid anymore.

Fear seemed a paltry emotion after the intense, primal madness that seized and shook her as Elan held her.

She cleared her throat. "Um, I can't seem to remember where I put my briefcase."

He gave her a quick look of alarm and pointed to where it lay at her feet.

"Thank you." She rifled inside it, bending forward and letting her hair hang down to conceal her crimson face. She pulled out a report she wanted to proofread and made a big show of finding her place and uncapping her pen.

She sneaked a glance at him. His expression was stony as he read his paper. He snapped the big pages open and scrutinized the tiny print with focused intensity. She attempted to concentrate on the dense scientific text in front of her, but her mind couldn't make sense of the words.

"I'm sorry." The words formed on her lips of their own accord.

I'm sorry I can't stop wanting you in just the way you despise.

"For what?" He didn't look up from his paper.

"For being a gibbering idiot. I had no idea I was going to react like that. I guess I'm officially a white-knuckle flier." She bit her lip. It was humiliating to see how little control she'd displayed in the face of fear.

"It's no matter," he said brusquely, without glancing up from the text. He snapped open another page, appeared to study it for a moment, then looked up. "There's no shame in showing fear of flying through the clouds."

His stony features softened as he looked at her. Sara swallowed hard as a strange surge of emotion threatened to overflow its boundaries. Fear, embarrassment and forbidden lust all roiled inside her, her poor nerve-racked body a fragile vessel for so much unfamiliar torment.

Poor Sara! He could see how greatly she suffered. She'd not betrayed even a moment of hesitation, had not mentioned her lack of flying experience until her fears overcame her as they boarded the aircraft.

Her obvious terror filled him with a powerful protective instinct that shook him to the core. He wanted nothing more than to put his arms around her and comfort her.

And the protective urge frightened him far more than any of the transient sexual thoughts that bedeviled him in her presence.

He'd left his home and his cruel father behind to build his own life, free of ties and obligations he had no use for. He needed no one and no one needed him—until he saw the fear that racked her delicate body and brought tears to her pale jade eyes. He couldn't sit and watch her suffer. And holding her was a pleasure beyond imagining. At his touch she softened and relaxed. Her shivering eased and her flesh warmed. She leaned into his embrace, welcomed his touch. Welcomed him.

Desire had seized him. Desire to offer her far more than comfort, to take far more than the satisfaction of soothing her fears.

He wanted to experience the sweet agony of her soft body pressed against his. To sink his fingertips into her lush curves. To fill her with the joy that swept through him each time she flashed her lovely smile in his direction.

And she was his for the taking. He could see that.

That knowledge alone should extinguish his desire.

"I bet you were a kid the first time you flew in a plane." Her voice startled him out of his tortured contemplation and forced him to refocus on the paper he'd been pretending to read.

"Yes, age eleven." He didn't dare look up. Those wide eyes cast a spell on him that right now he had no power to resist.

"Were you taking a vacation with your parents?"

A vacation? Did the concept even exist in his country? "No."

"Well?" Her lips twitched in a half smile as she waited for him to expand. Soft, delicate lips, thin and mobile.

That begged his mouth to close over them.

He struggled to wrench his mind back to her question about his first plane ride. And the memory it conjured dampened his feelings of pleasure.

"I left my home in Oman for the first time to fly to boarding school in England."

That day he'd left everything he knew, everyone he held dear, to find himself alone and afraid in a strange, cold country where no one understood his speech and customs. It had been a journey from which he would never truly return.

"Were you frightened?"

"Yes. Though perhaps not as you might imagine. I enjoyed the flight. Young boys take pleasure in the power of big machines." He forced what he hoped looked like a natural smile.

"Why did your parents send you away to school?"

Why indeed? Not so he could receive an excellent education, though that had been a result. Not so he could become familiar with the ways of western culture, though in time he had.

So his father could punish his mother. Rip her favorite child from her arms and banish him to a far land. Simply to show her that he could.

Anger still burned in his gut at the memory of his mother weeping as his father's aides dragged her screaming son away from her for the last time. Elan never saw her again. Her health was already frail—a neurological ailment—and after he was sent away her decline was swift, her death sudden.

And he could never forgive his father for taking her life as surely as if he'd slashed a knife at her throat.

He realized Sara was waiting for an answer to her question. "They thought it would turn me into a man."

That, too, was true. His father had reviled his close relationship with his mother. Abhorred how when he was little he'd liked to crawl into her bed to seek comfort from his nightmares, how he followed her on her daily rounds, laughing with her and the women, enjoying her gentle humor and loving caresses.

No son of mine will hide himself in the skirts of a woman! His father's words still rang in his ears.

"Leaving home so young must have been hard." Sara's voice trembled a little as she said the words softly. He realized she must be responding to emotion on his face. A twinge of embarrassment warred with an urge to tell her more.

"Yes. I spoke little English. I'd rarely been to the nearest city, let alone out of the country. I'd spent every day in the bosom of my family, and suddenly I was torn from all I'd ever known. Strange people, strange language, strange food and the English weather…"

Words poured from his tongue unbidden as Sara's kind eyes watched him. "I missed the bright sun of my home almost as much as I missed my family."

"I've heard the weather in England is a bit grim." She smiled tentatively.

"My horses were as surprised as I was. They couldn't understand why the sun had vanished and water kept falling from the skies. They at least enjoyed lush green grass."

"You took horses with you to boarding school?" Her eyes twinkled with curiosity and interest that only fired Elan's impulse to share memories he'd kept locked away for so long.

"Yes. I brought my two favorite stallions with me. The school insisted on gelding them. They said stallions couldn't run with the other horses."

The painful memory of his close companions being deprived of their manhood stung him. It seemed so symbolic at the time. The three of them together were humbled aliens in a strange land, stripped of their former power and position and all they knew. But together they'd found a way to survive. They'd learned a new language, figured out the rules and learned to play by them.

That long, hard exile from his country and from everyone he'd ever loved had made him into the man he was today.

"Aren't stallions supposed to be dangerous?" The innocent awe in Sara's eyes lifted the gloom descending on him.

"They must be handled with care. But a man who's ridden a stallion can never truly be satisfied with any other horse. To harness the feral power of the herd leader and to move with him as one is an experience like no other."

A delicate flush spread up across Sara's chin and cheeks. At first he was surprised, then he realized his words must have triggered a rather different image than the one he intended.

Perhaps she imagined how it would feel to ride *him*.

A smile tugged at the corner of his mouth as Sara's blush darkened a shade further.

To be sure, the image intrigued him, too.

The thought of her slim thighs squeezing him, her long, delicate fingers wound into his hair, her hips moving against him, urging him on—

Elan quickly rearranged his paper to cover his lap. His breathing was in danger of becoming audible and he struggled to focus his mind on something that would douse his desire.

Sara's lips parted as she wrenched her eyes from his face and rifled through her briefcase. Her skin flushed crimson right down to her blouse. Fair skin could be a terrible disadvantage. Her thoughts were literally written all over her face.

But he couldn't help wondering what other parts of her body might redden in response to his presence. Nipples blushing like ripe berries. The delicate flower of her sex a pink rose inviting him to taste its nectar, beckoning him to bury his face in its soft petals—

He cleared his throat loudly and rustled his newspaper. "Pardon me. Something in my throat." Mercifully his dark skin did not betray the sudden flush of heat surging though his body.

He was rock-hard, straining painfully against the zipper of his pants. He regretted removing his jacket, but if he rose to retrieve it from the seats on the other side of the aircraft, his situation would be very evident. Only the *Wall Street Journal* prevented his lust from being clearly visible to its instigator.

Why on earth did this woman have such an appalling effect on him? He felt like a man who'd wandered lost in the desert for months without water then stumbled across a glittering oasis. He gasped with hunger and thirst that had nothing to do with food and drink.

He'd not been celibate for the past decade. Women flung themselves at him on a regular basis, and sometimes he took what they offered. They had their needs, he had his. The enjoyment was mutual, the parting inevitable. Some of them sought a rich beau to pamper them, some of them an exotic lover to walk on the wild side with.

He could give them what they wanted without giving up anything of himself.

None of them saw the man inside. The simple man humbled by the poverty of his spirit. The lonely soul who had learned at the hands of his father that love and affection were crimes to be met with harsh and lasting punishment.

He was no longer capable of love and the knowledge did not even pain him anymore.

Well. That little train of thought had taken care of his erection nicely.

He flipped the page of his newspaper and sneaked a sidelong glance at Sara.

She'd fallen asleep?

Good.

He felt genuine relief for her. It would be far better for her to sleep quietly through their return to earth. The jolt of the landing would be a rude enough awakening.

Some of the client sites they visited had runways that tested the skill of the most experienced pilots. The site they were traveling to was remote, a new field, the runway probably still dusted with freshly turned soil. Even he sometimes became alarmed at the sight of rocky, uneven terrain rising up to meet the plane at high speed.

Quietly, he laid his newspaper aside. He didn't want its crinkling to rouse her from her peaceful slumber.

And she did look peaceful. Her delicate lashes rested against her cheeks. She did not wear mascara and her lashes were a soft, dark gold color, like the soil of his homeland.

Her cheeks were still flushed with pink, and her lips parted, moist, as if she'd just licked them.

And maybe she had.

What dreams danced in her head that caused her face to shimmer with a secret smile? A smile that didn't play upon her lips or sparkle in her closed eyes, but that lit her features with an inner radiance and made them glow with enchantment.

He didn't feel anything so mundane as lust for her at this moment. Her loveliness was a balm to his spirit.

And he respected her business acumen. She displayed an astonishing knack for putting clients at ease, for explaining complicated concepts without blinding business people with science, the way he tended to. He knew he often came off as pompous and standoffish. He wondered if she saw him that way. Probably. And she was probably right.

On their relatively short acquaintance he could see that Sara was a remarkable woman in many ways. A woman who deserved to be treated with respect. And as a mark of his respect he would not take advantage of her attraction to him.

Or his attraction to her.

He was a grown man. He could control his base instincts, rein them in the way he reined in the potentially dangerous power of the stallions he rode. She was a valuable employee. And he would do well to remember that when his primal urges threatened to get the better of him.

"Oh, God!" Jolted awake by a loud bang and a sudden jarring sensation, Sara couldn't remember where she was. "Did we crash?"

"No." Elan's eyes were on her as she opened her own. "We've landed. We're on the ground."

The plane shook and rattled, jarring Sara's rigid body as the wheels shuddered along the crude runway.

"Did I fall asleep?" Stupid question. Of course she had. Though how on earth that had happened she couldn't imagine. A response to sensory overload, perhaps? "Don't answer that."

Elan didn't look as if he had any intention of answering. Casual chitchat wasn't his style. An odd memory of singing with him crept into her consciousness. "Ninety-nine bottles of beer on the wall." Must have been a dream. Weird. And in her dream the singing was his idea. Weirder.

In a rush it all came back to her. Her humiliating display of terror as they'd boarded the aircraft. The way she'd practically hyperventilated as they taxied along the runway. How she'd clung to him as if he were a life raft in the open ocean.

She braced against her seat as the plane ground to an abrupt halt.

"Thank you."

She didn't know what else to say.

He merely nodded, folded his newspaper, and placed it in his briefcase.

Noise from the drilling rigs assaulted her ears as their driver parked the Jeep. She strained to hear Elan as he jumped out and beckoned her to follow. He strode toward the drilling site, enthusiasm evident in his energetic movements.

The heady aroma of crude oil filled the air. A phalanx of beam pumps stretched into the distance, rocking in a steady rhythm, pulling the oil from its age-old hiding place beneath the barren soil.

The oil field was a fairly recent discovery and Al Mansur Associates had bid aggressively for the contract to develop it. Sara had jumped at Elan's suggestion that she come see it.

But now as she stood amid the clamor and bustle of the job site, a twinge of apprehension twisted her gut.

She knew the theories behind supply and demand, soil mechanics, flow ratios. She understood drilling from a technical and economic standpoint. But now she wasn't sure she wanted to see exactly how the earth was plundered and forced to give up its secrets and riches.

Elan introduced her to the site foreman and they left their papers and briefcases in his office trailer. They donned safety glasses, hard hats and earplugs before he led them across the sandy soil and up a flimsy metal ladder onto a rig about to begin drilling.

The driller in charge gave Sara a stern list of warnings about where she could and couldn't stand, what to watch out for, the possibilities for injury if a piece of equipment broke or came loose, or the potential for a blowout if they found a shallow pocket of gas beneath the soil. By the time he'd finished, her nerves jangled as if she stood on a massive bomb that might explode at any moment.

She positioned herself as close to the giant drill as she dared. As it revved into action she imagined the dinosaur-like grinding teeth gnawing their way down through the rock below. Elan came and stood beside her, watching her reaction as the platform shook and shuddered with the movements of the machinery.

"This is my favorite part," he said, shouting over the motors.

"Typical male!" she shouted back.

Elan looked confused for a second then a slow smile spread over his face. He leaned toward her, as if to say something, so she removed her earplug, nerves jumping.

"You have a naughty mind." His lips brushed against her skin as he spoke and his voice resounded in the hollow of her ear canal, triggering a responsive rhythm that pulsed down through her body. The touch of Elan's lips on her skin was a sinfully sweet sensation.

Yes, I have a naughty mind. Since she'd come to Al Mansur Associates, her body seemed to have developed a mind of its own that had nothing to do with her intellect.

Elan's smile stayed plastered across his face. She could only begin to imagine what was going on in his mind as he watched the men guide the drill deeper and deeper into the earth.

When the drilling finally stopped, he placed his hand gently in the curve above her hips to guide her to the downward ladder. The simple and practical caress made her feel languid, sensuous.

"Is it a gusher?" she asked, half-joking, once they were back on solid ground.

"Not yet." He smiled. "Once they pump out the drilling mud it will be. But you won't see oil shooting up into the air. We don't like to waste a single barrel."

They spent the rest of the afternoon visiting wells in various stages of drilling and pumping. Elan moved about the job site with the ease and confidence of a man used to being in command. Honored that he'd chosen to groom her for a larger role in the company, Sara resolved to live up to his obviously high expectations of her.

Back on his private jet, he settled into the seat beside her. She wondered why he didn't sit in one of the other seats on the plane. There was no reason for them to sit together since they were the only passengers. Presumably he'd sat beside her on the trip out because she'd been clinging to him like a limpet.

Perhaps he wanted to be close in case she needed reassurance. Did she? Not about the plane. Now that she'd survived her first flight she was relatively relaxed about flying again.

She would like some reassurance that she could work with Elan without wetting his suit with her drool. And that kind of reassurance was not immediately forthcoming. Especially not as he removed his gold cuff links and—once again—rolled his shirtsleeves up over broad, muscled forearms.

Oh, dear. She pressed her fingertips to her eyelids. *Just don't look, okay!*

"Are you tired?"

"What? Er, yes. I suppose I am a little." Tired of the way she couldn't get a grip on her libido. "It was a fascinating day. I really appreciate you bringing me here."

"You're welcome. I've never brought my assistant out to the field with me before, but I can see your abilities are far above average."

"Thank you."

As the jet's engines roared to life, her gut clenched with sudden apprehension. Without a word he placed his hand over hers. But the warmth of his touch proved anything but soothing.

Fear evaporated as a painful lightning bolt of desire ripped through her, leaving a smoking trail of heat in its path. Her body burned with a dangerous and craven longing to become entangled with this man in a way that was entirely unprofessional.

Elan's hands were calloused. The rough texture of his palms made her skin prickle with awareness. His fingers were soft yet firm as they wrapped around hers. The unwelcome thought of those broad, masculine hands moving over her tortured flesh sent shock waves of agonizing arousal shivering through her.

Her feelings for him suddenly seemed like the oil pressurized beneath the earth, waiting to rush up and explode into the clear sky unless she kept them very carefully capped and sealed. And every second in Elan's presence brought her closer to a potentially devastating blowout.

Four

"Oh, I'm totally fine now that I've gotten used to flying," she'd said. "Really, I'm..." She turned to look out the window. "Oh."

She sat back in her seat quickly and pressed a hand to her chest. Elan glanced past her and saw the landing lights through the porthole window as the plane banked steadily to the right.

"Goodness, does it always tip to the side like that?" Her voice shook and she licked her lips anxiously.

"Yes, it's a normal part of the approach."

She pressed a hand to her mouth and slowly turned her head as the trail of lights twisted under the moving plane. Her knuckles whitened as she gripped the seat rest between them and he fought the urge to put his arm around her.

He wanted to warm her, soothe and caress her, soften her and then... *Typical male.* Her words at the site came back to him and he cursed himself. He'd assured her on her first day at the job that he was anything but typical, and he'd live up to that promise if it killed him.

She was seven years younger than him. She knew little of the world, as evidenced by the fact that she'd never been in a plane. He had a responsibility to himself, and to her, to make sure that nothing happened between them. He had a responsibility to Al Mansur Associates, which needed her sharp mind in its offices more than he needed her soft body in his bed.

The plane banked more sharply, turning in preparation for the final approach, and the twin rows of lights on the ground shone brighter and closer in the darkness. A tiny laugh emerged from her tightened throat. "People always see light coming toward them in their final moments, don't they?"

Instinctively he slid his hand over hers as those troubling protective instincts fired his neurons without asking permission. Her poor hand was so cold, her fingers gripping the metal armrest with grim determination.

"Don't worry, I've landed here probably a thousand times. This turn is a normal part of the…" His words trailed off as she slumped in her seat.

He immediately unbuckled himself and supported her head. He held her steady as the plane bumped down on the tarmac.

"Sara." He patted her cheek gently with his fingertips. "Wake up."

Her skin was ghostly pale, her soft lashes lowered, lips slightly parted.

Her breath was sweet on his face as he leaned into her. He allowed his lips to brush her skin as he whispered her name once again. Her cheek was the color and texture of a delicate rose petal. So soft under his lips, cool.

His memory tormented him with the image of Sara drinking in the aroma of the roses he'd given her in his office.

Those roses were nothing but clutter to him until that moment—dying things that mocked him with his own mortality.

But as she enjoyed their subtle perfume and admired their doomed loveliness, he had seen their beauty in a new light.

Lately he could see many things in a new light.

Sara was so unlike any other woman he had met. A bewitching blend of innocence and experience, candor and caution, she knew when to listen and learn, and when to take the reins and go her own way. A plain little thing? If only she were.

She didn't stir.

His arm brushed against her breast as he shifted position. The nipple tightened under her silky shirt in response to his touch. He sucked in a breath.

"Sara."

He stroked a strand of her golden hair away from her forehead, soft as fresh-spun silk. His fingers struggled with the urge to bury themselves in the fall of hair on her neck and his lips pulsed at the sight of hers, slightly parted as if waiting for a kiss.

The kiss of life?

She is breathing, fool. His urge to settle his mouth over hers had nothing to do with medical exigency.

Elan wheeled around as he heard the door to the cabin open.

"I hope the flight was satisfactory, sir. Good Lord, is she asleep?"

"She's fainted."

"But she's breathing?"

Elan nodded as the pilot strode across the cabin and leaned over Sara. His gut tightened as he watched the other man bend low over her body, close enough to enjoy her scent.

"She'll be fine." The aggression in his voice surprised him and caused the pilot to step back. "I shall carry her."

He took perverse pleasure in bumping the pilot roughly out of his path as he reached for her. He shoved his arms underneath her, steeling himself against the pleasure of touching her.

But no steel could withstand the torturous burden of longing that rocked him as her slender body fell against his.

"Sara." He uttered her name as a talisman against the forbidden desire that roiled in his belly. It must be a crime of some magnitude to lust after a woman who wasn't even awake.

Her eyelids fluttered. His heart constricted at the thought of those jade-and-gold eyes opening to meet his. He leaned his face closer to hers, his mouth almost touching the petal softness of her skin. "Wake up," he whispered.

Her lips parted and a rush of emotion and sensation shook him, making him glad his feet were firmly planted on the floor. He hugged her closer, fighting the urge to kiss her back to wakefulness.

"Er, Mr. Al Mansur, perhaps I should call an ambulance." The pilot's voice forced its way into his ears from a million miles away.

"That will not be necessary." Elan spat the words at him, irritated at the interruption. He wanted to watch his sleeping beauty awaken.

Sara's golden lashes fluttered again and her eyes sprang open. He felt his face crease into a broad smile as she looked at him in astonishment.

"What the...?" Suddenly her eyes were wide with fear and she kicked and struggled in his grasp. He wrestled to hold her still, not sure why, but enjoying it all the same.

"Put me down!" She writhed like a tiger cub and a huge chuckle welled up inside him and burst out as he lowered her to her feet.

"Gladly, madam."

She fussed over rearranging her suit and tucking her hair behind her ears. She looked around, obviously trying to get her bearings. "What are you grinning at?" The fire flashed in her eyes.

"I'm glad to see you awakened. And fiery as ever." He chuckled again.

She glanced quickly around the cabin. "We've landed."

"We have indeed," he said with mock gravitas. He could not help but enjoy her confusion. Feet planted apart, she stood poised to take on a host of attackers. He was almost tempted to throw a shadow punch and watch her spring at him like a tigress.

The pilot had opened the exterior door. "Perhaps we should help the young lady down the stairs. She may still be light-headed after her fainting spell."

"Yes, would you please carry our bags?" With one swift step Elan swept Sara off her feet and into his arms. He was unable to suppress another grin as she twisted and wriggled, struggling to free herself from his grip.

"Put me down! I can walk just fine."

"We'll take no chances. Your unconsciousness may have after-effects. I'll carry you to the ground as a safety precaution."

"This is ridiculous!"

Sara bucked against him, trying to loosen his grasp. He half expected her to bite him. He merely tightened his arms around her.

"Don't fight me. I'll put you down when we reach the ground," he reiterated. The throaty rasp of his voice surprised him. She gave him one last jab in the ribs with her elbow, which served only to widen his smile.

She jerked her head back to look him in the face. "Stop smirking!"

"Pardon me. I'm simply glad to see you alive and…kicking again." He bit back another chuckle.

Sara's lovely face creased into a frown. Somehow it tickled his funny bone more that she couldn't see the humor in the situation.

Her breath came in quick gasps and his blood surged along with hers as her heart pounded against his chest. Her eyelashes flickered against the harsh spotlight illuminating their descent to the ground. He knew she was shaken by what had happened, and that only fired the protective instincts tightening his arms around her slender body.

Slender, yet substantial. Muscled, taut, the body of a woman who knew how to fight for what she wanted.

And at that moment he knew far too well what he wanted. He was glad the blackness of the night hid the evidence of his desire.

Why on earth was she struggling in such a childish fashion? She could tell he found her resistance entertaining.

His arms had closed around her like steel bands, lifting her from the ground against her will. The urge to resist was instinctive, but hopeless against the solid mass of muscle that was Elan. How on earth a businessman came to be built like an ancient Olympian, she could not begin to imagine.

As she kicked and wriggled, his arms simply tightened more firmly around her in an embrace that clearly demonstrated his superior strength. Heat gathered low in her belly as the hard muscles of his torso crushed against her. His broad hands supported her with an ease that made her feel ridiculously feminine, and she struggled not to enjoy the odd primal pleasure of being gathered and held by such a powerful man.

At the bottom of the stairs he released her and settled her carefully on her feet. She stumbled back, burning hot, her heart slamming against her ribs, her limbs weak.

She was ready to get down on her knees and kiss the blacktop as she recalled the sudden rush of terror that had deprived her of her senses as the plane plunged toward the dark runway.

"Are you all right?"

"Yes." She forced out the lie.

"Can you walk to the car, or would you like me to carry you?" His throaty voice sounded deeper than usual.

Carry me.

"I can walk." Her voice emerged as a squeak.

She concentrated on putting one wobbly leg in front of the other as Elan took their briefcases from the pilot and strode to his long black sedan. He flung their bags in the back and helped her into the passenger seat before bidding the pilot good-night. Then he settled in behind the wheel and loosened his tie.

"Your address."

"What?"

"Where do you live? I need to drive you home. Unless you plan on walking."

"Oh, of course. Five-fifty Railroad Avenue. You take a right off Main." She wondered what Elan would think of her rather dingy apartment building. The salary he paid could buy her a nice house, but she had other financial obligations. Last week she'd made the first significant payments on her college loans and on her mother's gargantuan hospital bill, and that was a far greater concern than any luxury dwelling.

He drove away from the airport, silent. The dark roads were deserted, the moon dimmed by wispy clouds. Sara gasped as he braked hard.

"A coyote."

She saw the flash of reflective eyes in the headlights as the nocturnal creature studied them for a second before slinking off into the desert.

"Wow. That scared me."

"I'm sure the animal's fear was greater than yours. The twin moons of our headlights sweeping though the desert must be an alarming sight for the night creatures."

"I know how they feel. Apparently I haven't evolved along with the rest of Western civilization because my body didn't take too kindly to flying through the air. I'm sorry to cause such a scene at both ends of the trip."

"Don't worry about it." He turned to her and his warm smile made her suck in an unexpected breath.

Stop it, Sara!

Even the gentle pressure of her seat belt made her recall—

with a harrowing mix of remorse and pleasure—the far more insistent pressure of Elan's arms around her.

He'd removed his jacket to drive and his sleeves were rolled up. One big hand gripped the wheel, holding it steady as they ate up the long, straight road through the empty desert.

"I'm hungry," he announced, as they entered the neon-lit oasis of the town.

"Me, too." *In more ways than one.*

"Let's pick up something to eat. What would you like?"

"I don't know the restaurants. I haven't bought takeout since I've been here." *Trying too hard to squirrel away every penny.*

"The fried chicken is good. And the food at the Mexican place is always fresh."

Sara turned to look at Elan, who studied the neon signs with keen interest. Somehow it shocked her that he would eat takeout fried chicken like a regular person.

"Whatever you prefer."

"I believe I prefer steak fajitas." He turned to her with a raised eyebrow.

"Sounds good."

Yikes. As he pulled up she could see it was a drive-through. Did this mean she should invite him into her apartment to eat it? Or would he expect to drop her off with her dinner and return home to eat his?

Probably the latter.

He picked up their food at the drive-through window and handed it to Sara. Lord, she was hungry. The zesty aroma of grilled steak and onions filled the car and made her stomach growl. He chuckled.

"Your hunger is getting the better of you."

Don't I know it? She shifted in her seat, suddenly uncomfortable as she watched his broad hand settle over the gear shift and push it into Drive. She resisted the urge to fan herself or turn the air-conditioning on full as they pulled back onto the road.

"We must eat immediately. And I know just the spot." He sped through the town and back out into the desert.

Outside town he took a sharp turn toward the mountains. Shrubs and boulders along the roadside cast eerie shadows in the headlights. The road disintegrated into a dirt track as they climbed up toward the veiled moon and stars.

After only a few minutes he stopped the car and climbed out. Sara gingerly opened the door and lowered a foot onto the sandy ground of the dark desert. A match flared and she followed its glow to Elan. He'd opened the trunk and now lit a small fire a few yards from the car.

"What are you using for kindling?"

"Mesquite wood. I keep some in the trunk. The fire will keep animals from joining us for dinner."

Okay.

He spread a blanket on the ground while Sara retrieved their food and drinks from the car. The night was pleasantly warm and the fresh mountain air invigorated her tired body. The city lights twinkled below them in the wide valley like a carpet of jewels. Sara sighed with pleasure as she kicked off her shoes and settled on the blanket.

She unpacked their food and handed him his soda.

"Do you come here often?"

Oh, like that didn't sound stupid!

He chuckled. "I do."

"By yourself?"

Sara! Shove some food in your mouth to stop it flapping!

"Sometimes." His dark eyes flashed at her in the flickering firelight. The suggestion she read in them made her gut kick like a gun recoil.

It's all in your imagination!

Quickly she unwrapped her fajita and took a bite.

Elan sat cross-legged on the blanket. The glint of gold from his watch caught her eye as he unwrapped his own food. The strangeness of the situation struck her. She was seated by a fire in the midst of an empty desert, with a filthy-rich tycoon she had a massive and embarrassing crush on.

If my friends could see me now.

She sneaked a glance at him. He regarded her with a curious expression. Was he laughing at her? He hadn't started eating yet, and she hesitated before taking her next bite.

"After many years in England I like to begin a meal with a toast," he said. The fire flared, illuminating his face, where she read nothing but goodwill. "To you surviving your first plane flight." He lifted his soda cup and held it in the air. "Cheers."

She bumped her cup gently against his. "Cheers." She took a sip of her soda. The cool bubbles tickled her throat. "And my second plane flight. Though I only barely survived that one, didn't I?"

"Your response to the plane's descent was rather unexpected." His eyes twinkled with humor.

"Thank you for taking care of me." Her face heated as she realized she had no idea how she'd gone from being strapped in her seat to awakening in Elan's arms.

His dark eyes remained fixed on hers. "It was my pleasure." His husky voice and challenging stare sent her thoughts tripping over each other as they ran in a number of unseemly directions.

She took another bite of her fajita, trying hard not to think about him bending over her, lips poised mere inches from her own, his hands unbuckling her seat belt, loosening her clothing…

No, her clothing had not been loosened. *Earth to Sara!*

Elan did not seem the least bit preoccupied with thoughts of their rather eventful journey as he ploughed through three entrées with impressive gusto. She nibbled at her food and sipped her soda while she watched with amazement.

At last he looked up at her and wiped his mouth with his napkin.

"What?" A smile quirked at the corner of his mouth.

"Nothing."

"Rubbish. Your eyes are smiling. What's so amusing?"

"I've never seen anyone eat so much."

"I'm a man of prodigious appetites." He looked at her steadily, his head cocked.

I can imagine.

His lips twitched slightly, as if anticipating something other than eating. Sara suppressed a little shiver as her imagination started to work overtime.

"And we missed lunch today." His mouth creased into a smile. The flickering firelight danced over his proud features and made Sara's insides churn in a most disturbing way.

"Oh, yes, you're right. No lunch." She hadn't even noticed. Food was the last thing on her mind when Elan was around.

"I've been starving for hours."

Me, too.

He leaned back, braced himself on one powerful arm, and rested a hand on his belly. A belly as firm and flat as the desert floor, hidden by his white shirt. She knew exactly how hard it was since she'd been crushed against it only half an hour ago.

His hand was silhouetted against the pale cloth of his shirt, long fingers splayed. It was a hand that looked as though it could cradle the world in its palm. She could still feel his fingers on her flesh as if the heat of them had seared through her clothing and left a smoking imprint on her skin.

The fire sputtered and dimmed. Elan lifted himself and leaned across the blanket, reached past her to rearrange the mesquite strips. He knelt and rested his weight on one powerful arm—like a tiger ready to pounce—as he tended the blaze with one hand.

She struggled to keep her breathing inaudible as his torso almost brushed against her.

He blew on the flames and they flared. He pulled back and knelt beside her.

"This mesquite does not burn as steadily as camel dung." A wry smile curved his lips as he surveyed her with hooded eyes. She let out a laugh, glad of an excuse for a release.

"I guess it's not easy to find things to burn in the desert."

"You learn to make the most of what's at hand."

"Did you actually grow up in the desert?"

"Yes." He looked back into the fire. "We had a home in Muscat, the capital city, but my father usually went there on business alone."

"Do you miss your country?"

"Sometimes." He looked at her and an odd expression crossed his face. "It's a strange confession for me to admit that."

"Why?"

"I've lived here for many years. I left Oman at age twenty-one under circumstances that made me wish never to return." Hooded eyes gazed at the fire as his quiet, controlled voice mingled with the crackling flames. "I'm accustomed to a life of exile."

"Don't you miss your family?"

"My parents are dead." A flicker of emotion passed over his features and Sara battled the urge to ask more about them. It wasn't her place.

"Do you have siblings?" She couldn't imagine growing up without the companionship of her brothers and sisters. While her parents sniped at each other and tore each other down, her siblings had carried her through. She was the youngest and they'd brought her up to be the woman she was today.

Each of them had given up opportunities to help support the family and raise her after their dad had died. While they all wanted to help, she and her brother Derek were the only ones with enough income to make a serious dent in the debts from their mom's cancer treatments, and Derek had given up so much for Sara already. It was her turn to give back, and she'd better remember that when she was tempted away from the path of reason.

"I have two brothers." Elan glanced up from the fire, his eyes black, unreadable in the darkness. "I barely know them now."

The sadness in his voice clutched at her. He turned his head to look back at the fire and the flames danced over the hard edges of his profile.

"What are their names? Do they still live in Oman?" She wanted to draw him out, to learn more about him. But as his eyes met hers in surprise, her simple questions sounded like unseemly prying. Her stomach tightened. Once again she'd overstepped her bounds.

He looked at her for a moment, an oddly vulnerable expression in his eyes.

"My younger brother Quasar is a financier in New York. He's wild, the baby of the family. He was always getting into scrapes as a kid—challenging me to races on our father's priceless camels, hiding insects in the women's robes to make them scream." A smile flickered across his mouth. "He's still up to his crazy tricks, though now I read about them in the papers." His expression turned wistful, then serious as he leaned forward to tend the fire. "I'd like to see more of him, but we're both busy."

He brushed against her as he reached across the blanket and she sucked in a breath as a shiver of awareness fired her nerves. Sparks leapt as he blew softly on the wood. Sara struggled to pour sand on the sparks that crackled inside her as the tang of his alluringly male scent assaulted her in the night air, an exotic blend of soap, clean sweat, horses and expensive wool.

She wrenched her eyes from the powerful forearm revealed by his rolled-up shirtsleeve. Elan seemed mercifully unaware of the thrall he held her in as he settled back on the blanket.

"My older brother Salim took over from my father when he died."

"In the family business?"

"Yes." He wiped a hand across his mouth and looked out into the darkness. "I suspect he would rather have remained in

America." He glanced at her. "He came here for college—we all did. But he has a strong sense of duty and is not one to shirk his responsibilities. He's a good man, and again, a busy one. I grew used to being away from my family while I was in boarding school."

"Your brothers weren't sent to the same school?"

"No. Quasar went to school in Europe, Salim had a private tutor at home." Once again he leaned forward and blew on the fire, his angular features silhouetted against the halo of orange sparks that pierced the darkness.

As he rested the weight of his body on his strong arms she couldn't help a stray wish that he'd take her and hold her tightly, as he'd done when she fainted.

Get hold of yourself, Sara. You're just lonely—and your boss's arms are not the place to seek comfort.

"Does it take long to get used to being away from your family? I miss mine so much." Her voice cracked. "It's only been a month, I know, but…" She bit her lip, not wanting to cry. She was tired, emotionally overwrought after the long day.

"You've never been away from home before?"

She shook her head. She knew tears shone in her eyes as she looked at him.

The tender look in his eyes almost undid her completely. "I cried every night for a long time," he said softly. "I felt like a page ripped from a favorite story. A jumble of words and images that no longer made sense without its companions. In my country family is everything. We live very close, eat together, sleep together. To be separated from the people I spent all my days and nights with—I don't exaggerate when I say it nearly killed me."

"Oh, gosh." Tears pricked at her eyes and she shook her head, braced against a surge of emotions threatening to engulf her. "I can't even imagine how hard that must have been for you. At least for me it was a choice. I left because I wanted to make my own life."

"I understand." His low voice curled around her like smoke

from the fire, warming her. "I made that choice myself when I left my homeland again as an adult, to settle in America. In some ways it hurts more—you can blame no one but yourself for your isolation."

He shifted slightly, turned his head to gaze again at the flames. The flickering tongues of light danced over his features, obscuring them. "In time, a scab grows over even a self-inflicted wound."

But the haunted expression in his eyes belied his words. And in that moment she could see Elan's loneliness was a torment that would likely never leave him.

On instinct she reached out and touched his forearm. He jerked as if stung and she pulled her hand back but he deftly grabbed it and held it firm.

His eyes burned dark fire as he looked into hers. "Loneliness is the curse of man. Once he leaves his mother's womb he's doomed to wander the earth, seeking that comfort he once enjoyed."

He raised his fingers to her face and she gasped as he cupped her cheek with his hand.

"There is no comfort to be found, only solace." He said it slowly, his voice hushed.

She parted her lips to reply but no words formed on them. Her thoughts tangled and scattered to the desert wind as Elan's hot, urgent mouth closed over hers.

Her head tipped back as he leaned into her and seized her in his arms. Her moan escaped into his mouth as her hands flew to his neck.

His arms circled her torso, strong and hard as steel, vibrating with dangerous urgency. She shuddered with the intensity of her own longing, and with fear—of wanting too much, wanting more than could ever be given.

But fear evaporated in the desert air as Elan's arms embraced her. In his fierce kiss she lost herself and claimed the primal closeness her body and soul ached for.

Her skin hummed beneath her clothes as his hand burrowed under the jacket of her suit, fingertips pressing into the muscle of her back through her thin blouse.

She arched her back, bending like a willow under the force of his touch. They inched closer on the blanket, their bodies drawing together, meeting in new places as the distance between them diminished to nothing. Shoulders met, hips bumped, knees shuffled into each other as they wound their arms around each other, banishing any space that separated them.

Her fingers groped up into his thick hair, pulled him to her as their kiss deepened. He licked the inside of her lips. His hunger echoed through her and she gasped as he sucked her tongue.

His hand beneath her jacket tugged her shirt free from her skirt and slid underneath it. As his fingers touched her nipple through her flimsy bra, she shuddered at the stinging intensity of the sensation. Every nerve in her body sang a high-pitched note of quivering arousal.

Elan eased back on his haunches and pulled her over him until she sat with her legs wrapped around him, hugging him. His tongue teased her lips, licked and sucked, parted them gently, then pulled back. He eased her skirt up over her hips, roved over the fullness of her thighs with broad palms.

His fingers slipped inside her panties and played over her backside, squeezing and testing. Her body opened up to him, soft and warm and wet, wanting him. She pushed her breasts against his chest, her nipples straining for contact with the hard muscle.

And, oh, how she wanted him. Her skin smoked under his touch, her blood heated, her whole body burned to be consumed in his fire.

He jerked his head back and licked the outside of her lips with exquisite gentleness. Then he shoved his tongue deep into her mouth with deft and daring ease. Her body bucked at the suggestion and a soft groan escaped her.

She buried her face in his neck, inhaled the intoxicating feral scent of his skin. She cupped his face with her hands, let her fingers explore the hard edges of his jaw, enjoy the cut of his cheekbones, rove into the softness of his hair.

Elan.

Elan!

What on earth was she doing?

She yanked her head back and forced her eyes open, her body literally shuddering with desire as she struggled to regain control.

His eyes opened slowly and the flickering firelight danced in their black depths.

"I want you, Sara. And I know our need for each other is mutual." The low rumble of his voice was a distant earthquake that shook her and crumbled any remnants of reason.

"Yes."

Five

She pulled him closer, settling her mouth over his as she surrendered to forces far stronger than good sense. Crackling bursts of electrical energy shot through her as their tongues touched.

She showered his face with kisses. His closed eyelids flickered under her lips as she dusted his skin with their caress. Her lips tingled as she relished the roughness of his cheeks.

Elan's hands were not idle while she tasted the salt of his skin and grazed the hard line of his jaw with her teeth. He tugged down the zipper on her skirt, sucked in a sharp breath as she gently bit his earlobe.

Her breasts quivered under her blouse as he pushed her gently away from him and undid the buttons of her jacket. He eased it off over her shoulders then tackled the buttons of her blouse with the same careful concentration.

The pause gave Sara time to think about what she was doing. Or what she wasn't doing. Shouldn't she be clutching her blouse, leaping to her feet and running for the sanctuary of the car? *What good could come of sleeping with my boss?*

But at that moment she could no longer see Elan as the boss. The long, powerful fingers carefully tugging at her tiny pearl buttons were those of a man—just a man—who wanted to hold her as much as she wanted to be held by him, and who wasn't afraid to say it.

The moon emerged from behind a bank of clouds, and anticipation shone in his dark eyes, reflecting her own.

His breathing hitched as he parted her silk shirt to reveal her breasts. Her cream lace bra lifted and offered them like fruits ripe for plucking.

She watched as he slowly raised his hands to touch them. The soft curves of flesh thrilled as his fingertips neared them. Her nipples tickled under the scratchy lace, begging to be touched. As if her tortured flesh communicated directly with him, Elan softly tugged at the lace edging the cups until her breasts spilled into his hands.

Sara released a sigh as those broad hands settled over her breasts, kneading them gently as he claimed her mouth with a kiss.

Heat flooded her limbs and she pressed herself against him, rubbed her hips against his hard belly, enjoyed the strength of his arousal through his clothes.

She wanted him inside her.

The ache of loneliness that followed her everywhere had transformed into a raging inferno of longing to connect with this man. Knowing that he, too, felt alone, needing someone—needing her— she knew they would fit together like two parts of a broken whole.

She fumbled with his belt, struggling to free the stiff leather from its loops, as his muted groans filled her ear. His tongue teased her earlobe and sent shivers of sensation sizzling up and down her neck as she tugged at the zipper on his pants and pushed them down over his hips.

She pulled at the buttons on his shirt in her urgency to bare his chest. His skin shone dark bronze in the flickering firelight, but unlike hard metal it felt hot and responsive to her touch.

She trailed her fingers over the ridges of muscle as she pushed his shirt back over his shoulders and he shrugged it off.

"I must get protection," he whispered.

Her eyes widened. The idea of protection had not even crossed her mind.

She gasped as he pulled back. It literally hurt to part from him even for a few seconds. He stepped out of his remaining clothes before he headed back to the car. Naked.

His body was magnificent. The full moon bathed the land in pale silver light. Elan looked like a god walking the earth as he strolled barefoot, dusted with moonbeams, over the rough desert soil.

He opened the passenger door and reached into the glove compartment, then slammed the door and strolled back to her. His easy, rolling gait belied his massive build. Every part of him was big. Big hands, strong arms, thickly muscled torso and powerful legs that carried him back to her in a few long strides.

His arousal was undiminished and hers only intensified by the agonizing separation from his blood-heating presence. She welcomed him back into her arms, gripped him too hard, not wanting to be parted from him again.

She lay back on the blanket and pulled him over her almost roughly. She craved his strength, his steadiness, the raw masculinity of him. Sandwiched between the hard ground of the desert and Elan's hard body, she writhed at the blissful torture. And she wanted to feel his hardness inside her.

He rolled back to rip open the packet and sheath himself. With careful fingers he touched and probed her moist folds and parted them. He eased himself into position over her, teased her painfully aroused flesh with the tip of his penis. Then he entered her.

He sank in, but so slowly she thought she'd go out of her mind with the agonizing pleasure of it. He lowered his body into hers and their skin met as they came together, inside and out, circling each other with arms and legs, mouths meeting and breath mingling in the moment of glorious unity.

Elan sighed softly in her ear as his body settled into hers. A perfect fit.

She could feel him quickening inside her. The sensation made her gasp and laugh and her eyes sprang open and met his steady gaze. His eyes sparkled with joy and a smile teased at the corners of his mouth. His lips parted as if to speak or shout or moan, but he lowered his head and buried his face in her neck, clutching her with his hands.

"I've never felt such desire for a woman," he breathed hot in her ear. She gasped as again she felt him move inside her. "I've never wanted…never needed…" His words were lost in a grunt of pleasure as he moved and shifted, deepening and strengthening the bond between them.

They worked together, hips lifting, bellies rolling over each other, legs and arms hugging and gripping as they moved together toward the ecstasy they craved.

They writhed on the blanket, the solid earth supporting them as she gave herself over to an intensity of sensation, a sheer, wringing pleasure she could never have imagined.

Elan's lovemaking was exquisite. Tender and loving, harsh and demanding, he rode her and fought her, caressed and comforted her, kissed and licked and teased and tormented her. Every inch of her skin, every cell in her body, sang with the clear, mad beauty of love.

Love?

Yes. Surely only love could upend the universe and shake it until stars rained down on them. And that love filled her now until she brimmed with explosive wonder, sheer joy that threatened to burst and shatter her into a thousand pieces.

His hot breath tickled her ear. "Sara, I... I..." She never knew what he struggled to say because at that moment he exploded inside her, shuddering and quaking with the force of his release as her own climax seized her and swept her into a vortex of agonizing bliss.

Elan's hand rested gently on her cheek as they lay side by side. They were both spent, exhausted, and Sara's body hummed with calm joy in the aftermath of their lovemaking.

He shifted closer, until his belly pressed against hers. He stroked her hair softly and placed a gentle kiss on her cheek. When his stomach tensed, she expected him to say something, but he didn't. Perhaps he wanted to but couldn't find the words. She certainly had no words for what had happened between them.

She could tell he didn't want to let her go. He didn't want to break the delicate bond that held them together. Maybe he, too, felt whole, warm, safe, blissfully free of rational thoughts and tiresome practicalities. Out there on top of a bluff, with nothing between them and the pale moon, they were the only people on earth.

But the fire had gone completely out and her skin tingled at the thought of all the wild creatures moving around them. Coyotes, bobcats, lizards...rattlesnakes. A rustling in the sand close by made her flinch. They might be the only humans, but they most definitely were not alone.

"We'd better go before something comes and bites us," she said reluctantly.

He nibbled her ear playfully. "You're in great danger of being bitten by me. Anything else that tries to taste your loveliness will have me to answer to."

She wriggled against him. It was easy to imagine Elan taking on any earthly creature. He radiated strength and self-confidence that surely even the most determined scorpion would shrink from.

"But you're right, my beauty. We must go."

They exchanged a last gentle kiss before tearing themselves away from each other to gather up their scattered clothes.

As they climbed back into the car, Sara knew they were leaving the magical world they'd inhabited. The click of the seat belt seemed symbolic of the return to a world of rules and regulations.

Elan's shirt hung unbuttoned over his pants, and she longed to reach over and touch his chest as he drove. But she knew better. The time for carefree touches and playful intimacy was over. Her gut tightened as a surge of apprehension replaced the carefree ease she'd enjoyed only minutes ago.

A dark mood had settled over him. He looked straight ahead as he drove, his face stony in profile. She tried to think of something to say, a casual conversational gambit to break the tension thickening the air, but no words seemed appropriate to the strangeness of the situation.

What could she say? *Thanks, that was fun! Gosh, the desert's lovely at night, isn't it? We'd better get some sleep, we've got an early meeting tomorrow!*

Gulp.

She froze in her seat as the reality of the situation crept over her like icy fingers.

She'd slept with her boss.

No, not true. She hadn't slept with him. She'd clawed his back, howled in ecstasy, pushed her hips against his and ridden him, clung to him and moaned his name in the throes of her orgasm.

Oh, dear.

Perhaps if they were now sitting there chatting about what movie they'd go see on Saturday night it would seem, well, not normal, but okay. But the way he gripped the wheel, his jaw clenched, eyes narrowed, lips pressed together, she could see that tonight was not the first night of an ordinary dating relationship.

As if this kind of night ever could be. What man would want

a girl who "put out" on the first date? And it wasn't even a date. He'd offered her dinner and she'd thrown herself at him.

She was no virgin. She'd had a boyfriend in high school and another in college. But she'd never in her life slept with a man she wasn't "going steady" with. "If you don't respect yourself…" She could hear her oldest sister Nathalie's cheerful voice in her ear. The lecture had been given in a playful tone since no one expected Sara to need it anyway.

Then she'd met Elan. He undid her in a way that was truly frightening. That stripped away the thin layer of civility to reveal her primitive core.

Neon lights flickered on the main drag as they drove back into town. Dawn hovered behind the hills and the purple sky threatened to explode into blazing sunlight at any moment.

"Take a left here."

His big hands slid over the wheel as he turned into her apartment complex.

"Would you like to come up for coffee?" She almost choked on the words but it felt only polite to offer. She would love for him to come up. To talk and break the chill silence that had settled over them like dew on the desert.

"I think we should both get some sleep," he said softly. He pulled the car to a stop outside the front door. For the first time since they'd climbed into the sedan, he turned to look at her.

The faraway look in his dark eyes touched a raw place in her, summoned her. She wanted to touch him. She wanted to close the distance echoing between them even in the cramped space of the car.

She ached to be held in his arms.

He opened his mouth—to speak, or to kiss her?—but he didn't move. And then his mouth closed, full lips settling together, as if they'd already said everything there was to say.

She wanted so badly to kiss him goodbye. To press her lips

against his skin one last time, to feel the heat of his blood warm her mouth. But the rigid set of his shoulders and the high angle of his chin warned her off. No kisses were offered by either party.

"Good night, Sara."

"Good night, Elan." Her voice trembled a little and she thought she saw a flicker of emotion in his eyes. But perhaps it was just a reflection of her own confusion and embarrassment as she fumbled for her briefcase on the floor. She scrambled out of the car, clutching her crumpled clothes around her.

The big sedan didn't move until she'd gone inside, so she never actually heard him drive away. But she suffered his leaving as a limb being torn from her body. If she'd felt alone before, now she felt desolate, destitute. Like Eve banished from Paradise because she couldn't keep her hands off the tempting and dangerous fruit within.

Sara operated on automatic pilot as she parked her bicycle and walked into the office building the next morning. She knew Elan wouldn't be there yet, since she always arrived early enough to change into professional attire and get her desk organized before the day got hectic. He didn't usually come in until around nine.

As nine o'clock drew closer she found it impossible to concentrate on her work. Her blood thundered audibly in her head, her heart banged against her ribs, and she kept catching herself nervously drumming a pen on her desk.

Oh, God. What would they say to each other? *Hi. Good morning. Can I get you anything? Like me, naked on a blanket in the moonlight?*

She cringed inwardly. She was preparing a complicated report with multiple columns of figures and the numbers jumped and buzzed before her eyes like performers in a flea circus.

Each time the doors to the elevator opened she fought an urge to dive beneath her desk like a creature startled to its burrow. Just the mail clerk. The assistant from finance with some new figures. Each arrival sent her into a frenzy of panic.

When a messenger arrived with a small box wrapped in gold paper, Sara's eyes widened. Had Elan sent her something? She leaped out of her chair to receive it, a smile rising to her lips.

"Thanks!"

She ripped open the card with trembling fingers.

"Mr. Al Mansur, thanks for all you've done for us in Alberta. In eager anticipation of another banner year, yours, Tony Leon, Acme Drilling Co."

It wasn't for her. It was for Elan. A corporate gift. Probably another set of gold-plated golf tees.

Sara sagged with misery. How pathetic that she'd so quickly assumed Elan had made a romantic gesture.

Wishful thinking.

She put the box in his office and returned to her chair to resume her anxious vigil.

But he didn't come in.

By noon she was confused and upset. He'd missed an important meeting with a supplier, yet had not asked her to take his place in it. Apparently he'd phoned his regrets to the other attendees.

"When is he coming?" asked first one caller, then another and another.

"I'm not exactly certain," gradually became a mumbled, "I don't know," as Sara's professional demeanor slipped a little further with each admission. She maintained his schedule, made all his appointments and usually knew his movements better than he did.

She was tempted to call his home to see if he was okay. But he'd excused himself from the meeting so he was obviously alive. He'd simply chosen not to come into the office today.

Had chosen not to see her.

"When's Mr. Al Mansur coming back from Turkey?"

"What?" Sara glanced up from her work, anxiety spiking in her gut.

The Assistant VP for Production stood in front of her desk, a pen pressed to her carefully made-up lips. "It's just that I really need him to sign these documents. I had no idea he was leaving for Turkey today."

"Me neither." Despair descended in a heavy fog. He'd left the country without telling her?

"Are you okay?" The other woman's concern wrinkled her smooth brow as she hugged her thick folder of documents to her chest.

"Sure." The word emerged excessively loud as she tried to exude self-confidence she didn't feel. "I'm not sure when he'll be back," she said more quietly. She didn't even know which airline he'd taken. He must have bought his own ticket.

"Is he there to look over the El Barak field? The one where the wells needed deepening?"

"I expect so." She struggled to sound as normal as possible. "I'll let you know as soon as I hear from him."

"You don't look well. Are you sure you're okay?"

"Yes. Just a slight headache, I'll take an aspirin for it."

She rested her head on her desk as the door closed behind her coworker. A woman ten years older than herself and in a position of considerable authority. She was everything Sara hoped to be herself: respected, liked and admired for her quick thinking and effective teamwork.

That could have been her in a few years. *If I hadn't slept with my boss.*

If only she could take an aspirin for heartache.

Elan was gone for four days. She spoke to him twice on the phone and their conversations were entirely professional. He wanted some documents e-mailed to him. He advised her of his return flight. She reported the minutes of a meeting he'd missed.

There was no mention, or even suggestion, of what had happened between them.

Sara was sure she would be terminated as soon as he returned. After all, she'd promised that if she didn't perform as agreed— including keeping her eyes and hands off the boss—he could fire her outright. With that promise she'd slammed the door on any sexual harassment lawsuit.

She attempted to polish her résumé, but realized she couldn't even include this job on it if she'd been here only one month. It would be obvious she'd been fired.

She wondered if she could beg him to keep her on for a few more months, just until she could find something else. She wondered if she could brazenly insist on holding her job, as she'd done on the first day.

It takes two to tango.

Even if she'd been warned from the outset that tangoing with the boss was strictly not on the agenda at Al Mansur Associates.

"Good afternoon, Sara." Elan swept past her like a gust of wind, blowing through the doors from the elevator and into his office. His door slammed behind him before her brain fully registered his presence.

She hadn't even managed a polite greeting.

Her pulse pounded in her temple as she dragged herself to her feet. She picked up a big stack of papers and a long series of messages she'd collected. There was nothing for it but to go in. Might as well get it over with.

She hesitated, held up her trembling fist for a moment before rapping on the door. Should she say anything about what had happened? Attempt a preemptive apology? She'd have to play it by ear. Ears almost deafened by the blood thundering in her head.

She knocked.

"Come in."

The door swung open to reveal Elan seated in his leather throne. He looked up as if startled, though he must have known it would be her. He sprang to his feet and ran a broad hand through his hair.

"Sara."

She gulped. "Yes."

He looked right at her and she froze, turned to stone. His eyes were narrowed in a penetrating gaze, black and shadowed, his face taut, jaw clenched.

"I feel I must offer my most humble apologies for the events of last week."

Her gut seized and she held her breath.

"You are a valued employee here. I think it's best if we do not mention those events again."

Thoughts rushed her brain and swept around in mini-cyclones—*he isn't firing me.*

He wanted to forget their night together.

The rush of relief at getting to keep her job was undercut by a harsh stab of humiliating disappointment. Had she really expected to continue some kind of intimate relationship with Elan? Even after he disappeared for days, fled to the other side of the world to avoid her?

The ache in her heart told her she had.

"Yes," she whispered. Her voice emerged as a hiss of steam released from an overheated radiator, but she was relieved she could find it at all. "Thank you."

She could almost swear she saw him flinch as she said "thank you." Was he disgusted that she didn't resign on principle? Someone wealthy like him probably couldn't understand how you could need a job more than your pride.

He nodded curtly. She cleared her throat and attempted to give him his messages in as normal a voice as possible.

He listened politely and responded appropriately, but as she talked she could see him looking almost anywhere but at her. A muscle worked in his jaw and his shoulders were rigid with tension. His discomfort in her presence was obvious.

And he had good reason to be uncomfortable. Because even as she spoke, her mind wandered. Wondered. Remembered the feel of his hands on her. Remembered the scent of him as she buried her face in his neck. Remembered the sweet, soothing warmth of being held tightly in his arms.

He studied a document, following the lines with his finger. The finger that had traced a line from her chin, to her belly button, to her agonizingly aroused… She blinked and swallowed hard, trying to shove down the disturbing sensations creeping through her body.

What was it about this man that made her professional demeanor fly out the window? That unhinged her almost to the point of madness?

She tore her eyes from him and tried to focus on the papers on his desk, on the spectacular expanse of clear sky visible through the window, on the spotless gray carpet. But each time her attention drifted back, in imperceptible degrees, to the man who consumed it.

To the way his hair was starting to touch his collar slightly in the back, in need of a cut. To the powerful tanned wrists revealed by the turned-back cuffs of his white shirt. To the way his tie was loosened slightly, accommodating one opened button at the neck of his shirt. Elan always looked a little too confined in clothes, as if he'd like to peel them off and get comfortable.

Or was it just her that wanted to peel them off? The thought made her anything but comfortable. She closed her eyes, attempting to block the sight of him from her vision. To block the image of him from her mind. But his midnight gaze was burned into her retinas.

"Are you...all right?"

"Yes," she said, her voice rather too high-pitched. He might well ask. He'd caught her standing in his office with her eyes closed. Was she all right? *Most definitely not.* She wasn't sure if she'd ever be all right again. "Will that be all?" She managed to plaster on a thin veneer of professionalism, even as she started automatically backing toward the doorway.

"Yes, thank you." Elan had turned away from her and bent over his desk, opening a drawer. She could see his biceps flexed tightly under the cotton of his shirt, his fists almost clenched. The tension in the air was suffocating, a cloying atmosphere of regret and recrimination that tormented them both.

What on earth had she been thinking when she touched Elan, when she kissed him, when she...

She turned on her heel and flew out the door. She accidentally slammed it in her haste to escape. Outside, she gasped a deep gulp of air and bent double as blood rushed to her head.

The only way she could survive this was to pretend it had never happened. To avoid thinking about it. *It.* The elusive *it* that sprang only too readily to the forefront of her consciousness. A night against which all other nights would inevitably be measured for the rest of her life.

Six

"We'd be delighted to do business with you. Thank you so much for coming." Sara shook the last cool hand of the venture capitalist team from New York. She ushered them out of the conference room, professional smile fixed in place.

As the tall mahogany door closed behind them she collapsed into a chair, shaking.

A six-hour meeting. With the CEO, CFO, new business strategist and two administrative staff.

By herself.

"I'm sure you can handle the details," Elan had said, when he announced he had other plans that morning.

Anderson Capital, which planned to invest in small "wildcat" oil-drilling firms and employ El Mansur Associates' technology and expertise to make them more profitable, had the potential to bring millions of dollars of annual revenue to the company. And Elan had handed her the account, to win or lose, all on her own.

He wanted her to fail.

He wanted her to admit defeat. Quit. Leave.

And he wanted that so badly that he didn't mind risking an important account to do it.

She'd already failed once. She'd betrayed his trust, broken her promise that she would not overstep the bounds of her job. This time she was determined not to fail.

Every day her mountain of responsibilities increased. The challenges Elan tossed in her direction grew more complex and demanding. She hadn't slept more than three hours a night lately as she needed every single minute to prepare for the onslaught of meetings, reports and presentations that were now her responsibility in addition to her administrative duties.

Her cell phone vibrated—again—and she thought of the work that must be piling up on her desk right this minute.

She took a deep breath. "Hello."

"Please come to my office." Elan.

A flash of anger warred with the heat his deep voice conjured as it curled into her ear. "I'll be right there." How could he push her this hard?

She hung up the phone, gathered her papers, and shoved out into the hallway.

This is what she wanted, right? A challenging, highly paid position in the exact field of her expertise. Of course she'd never dreamed she'd be performing duties more suited to a senior vice president than to an executive assistant and project manager. She had Elan to thank for that, though thanks was really the last thing on her mind right now.

She stormed out of the elevator on her floor, dropped the sheaf of papers on her desk—which now looked as overloaded and messy as Elan's—and rapped on the door to his office.

"Come in."

She steeled herself against the sight of him.

"How was the meeting?" He lounged back in his chair. His black gaze threatened to steal the breath from her lungs as she groped for a response.

"I believe it went well," she said stiffly. "They were concerned specifically about our ability to scale production quickly in the event a large new field was discovered, and I assured them that would not be a problem."

"Good. I'd like you to prepare a proposal that covers any issues raised during the meeting and provides them with a detailed summary of the services we can offer..."

She nodded, watching his mouth as he rumbled about the chain of production and pipeline capacity.

Was this the same man who had held her that night in the desert?

She'd looked into his eyes and felt a connection deeper than she could have ever imagined. He'd held her so tenderly, so passionately, she was sure she'd found...her soul mate.

She'd been wrong.

She swallowed hard. "I'll have it on your desk first thing tomorrow."

He regarded her steadily for a moment, dark gaze drifting over her face. Could he see she was exhausted? Barely able to function?

Did that give him satisfaction?

She could read nothing in his stern features.

As his fingers wrapped around his gold fountain pen, she couldn't help but remember the way they'd circled her waist, his hands so broad and strong he could lift her as if she weighed no more than a grain of sand.

"Thank you," he said. Her dismissal. He turned back to the report he was reading.

She stood her ground. *You won't break me.*

She stared at him for a moment, daring him to look back up at her. Did she imagine it, or did his fingers tighten around the pen? He paused in his reading, tugged at his collar, then glanced at her.

Their eyes met. "Will that be all?"

Sir.

She wanted him to know she saw the game he was playing.

"Yes, Sara." He said her name slowly, emphatically, his dark eyes unblinking. Her stomach flipped and she held herself steady.

His full lips straightened into a hard line.

Lips that had kissed her with force and tenderness she could never have imagined. Lips that had teased and tempted her into a frenzy of passion.

Lips that held the power to fire her, as she'd invited him to do on her first day.

Yes, she'd failed once, and she wanted him to know it would *never* happen again.

Elan leaned back in his chair and let out a long, hard breath as the door closed behind her. The woman was stubborn as a camel and twice as tough. Any normal person would have thrown in the towel, but Sara?

Nooo.

He couldn't help the smile that sneaked over his lips. This small woman had the courage of ten men. Unfortunately, she had the intelligence and aptitude of ten men, too, so no matter how much work he threw at her, somehow she managed to get it done. He was beginning to wonder if a little man called Rumplestiltskin visited her apartment in the evenings.

No. There was no time for any man in her evenings. He'd seen to that.

He wiped the smile of satisfaction from his face. Her evenings were no concern of his.

He'd made an error of judgment—once.

She'd touched something inside him he'd thought buried and forgotten. Reopened old wounds he was sure had scarred over.

She'd seen past the strength, past the power, past the money—
to the man within.

He'd felt, that night, that he *needed* her.

He rose from his chair, anger flaring in his chest.

He needed *no one,* and he would *never* let that happen again.

Seven

Bent over the sink in the office bathroom, Sara suffered another sudden surge of nausea. She was exhausted, drained, run-down.

And more than three months pregnant.

Until her visit to the doctor that afternoon, the possibility of a pregnancy had never crossed her mind. She'd bled after all, just not as much as usual, and the bleeding never really seemed to go away. She'd felt ill from time to time, but she'd put it down to stress and lack of sleep. After what seemed like a few weeks of intermittent on-and-off period she went to her gynecologist.

Diagnosis: Pregnancy.

The bleeding was abnormal and her doctor's concern showed in her face. Sara had no idea what showed on her own face: astonishment, disbelief, possibly horror.

She was bustled into an ultrasound room and unceremoniously stripped and smeared with gel so the bizarre events taking place inside her could be examined in scientific detail.

All disbelief vanished when she saw it on the ultrasound monitor. *My baby*. Its little heart pumping visibly, its tiny limbs already distinguishable, curved under its big head.

Her panicked gasping had frightened the ultrasound technician.

"Don't worry, dear," the nurse said softly. She was soft all over, from her gloved hands to her fluffy blond hair. "The uterine environment looks quite normal. Some people do continue spotting for some weeks with no known cause. There's no apparent danger to your pregnancy."

Her reassuring words penetrated Sara's consciousness, but they only made tears rise in her throat. A turmoil of unfamiliar emotions racked her body. Guilt that she hadn't spared a thought for the "uterine environment." A fearful recoil at the alien life secreted in her belly for so long without her knowledge. And— even more alarming—a fierce tug of intense affection for the tiny person growing inside her.

She stumbled back to the office to prepare a report for a meeting the following morning. It hadn't occurred to her to do otherwise. That was before the reality of the situation sank in. Before she found herself sitting at her desk, unable to focus her eyes, confused thoughts crowding her brain and terror twisting her gut. Before she sprinted into the bathroom, overwhelmed by nausea and the horrifying reality that everything in her life was about to change.

Had already changed.

She couldn't keep working this hard. She was endangering not only her health, but that of her baby. The report for tomorrow's meeting would have to wait. She'd apologize, say she was ill. But she'd sneak out and call in her regrets from home because she just couldn't face Elan right now.

She wasn't sure if she could ever face him again.

All his cruel assumptions about her on her first day had proven horrifyingly accurate. She had lusted after him and seduced him.

She'd risked the career opportunity of a lifetime for a few hours of pleasure.

Gambled with her life for one night in his arms.

And I am carrying Elan's baby.

The thought hit her for the first time like a splash of icy water. Somehow in the terrible excitement of discovering she was pregnant she'd managed not to think about the other person responsible for the life growing inside her.

How would he react? With shock, most likely. With horror, no doubt. Her disgrace was total.

She quickly stripped off her suit and put on her cycling clothes and sneakers, then shoved her suit into her backpack with far less care than usual. It wouldn't fit for much longer anyway.

She splashed her face with water and pulled her hair into a ponytail. Her eyes were red and her skin blotchy with distress. Hopefully she could get away without running into anyone.

She emerged from the bathroom and dashed for the elevator. She hugged herself, struggled to keep her breathing even, to keep tears at bay until she left the office.

But the elevator arrived with Elan inside it.

He strode out, then paused. "Sara, you don't look well."

"Yes." Her voice emerged as a whisper.

Guilt and terror paralyzed her limbs. Her secret swelled inside her, threatening to inflate like a giant blow-up and knock her over.

"Perhaps you're working too hard?" He raised an eyebrow.

"Um…" She couldn't seem to formulate a sentence that didn't contain the words *I'm having your baby.*

I've got to get out of here.

A massive surge of adrenaline flooded her limbs with the urge to shove past him into the elevator and escape. Her heart thundered as she zeroed in on the dimly lit cavern that was her only escape route. If she could just get in there and let those doors close behind her.…

Elan stood barring the way, his brow lowered with concern.

"You're ill. You should not ride your bike. I'll drive you home."

"No!" She spat the word, as images of their last car ride together assaulted her. *Elan, shirt unbuttoned to reveal his hard chest. His broad hand on the wheel.*

His sperm swimming toward her egg.

"I'll be fine. The exercise will do me good. Do you mind if I…" she stammered, able to focus only on the dark emptiness of the elevator that would carry her away from a drama she wasn't ready to take her part in.

He stood aside. Was that relief on his face? "We have no matters that can't wait until tomorrow."

"Thanks." She dove past him. He let go of the elevator door he'd been holding for her. She saw him turn and look at her, his brow furrowed, as the doors closed.

She sagged against the cold metal walls as the elevator hummed into motion.

Oh, I'm not ill. I'm just pregnant with your child.

"You're kidding me," said Erin, after a very long pause. Her sister was the first person she'd called. As a single mother herself, Sara figured Erin would be able to relate.

"Would I kid about something like this?" Sara paced back and forth in her small apartment, trying not to bump her hip on the kitchen countertop or pull the phone off the wall. She couldn't keep still. Too jumpy.

"You're pregnant? By who? You only just moved there and you weren't dating anyone here. Or were you?"

"No. I haven't dated anyone since I broke up with Mike last year." She paused to look out the window. The sun was sinking behind the mountains; soon the town would be plunged into darkness. She swallowed hard, twisted the phone cord in her hands. "I slept with my boss."

"Your boss? I thought your boss was the owner of the company."

"Yes," she rasped. It sounded even worse out loud than it did in her head.

"Isn't he some millionaire oil tycoon?"

"Yes." She closed her eyes.

"Is he, like, fifty years old or something?"

"No, of course not. He's thirty-two." And handsome. And irresistible.

And he despises me.

"So, jeez, is this like, a relationship?"

"No." She tugged at the phone cord, her eyes starting to sting. She bit the inside of her mouth to stem any tears. "It was a one-night thing. A mistake."

She heard Erin blow out a deep breath. "Wow. That's just so…not like you."

"Tell me about it. I've worked my butt off to get this job, and you know how much we need the money. But there was something about him…" Her voice trailed off and she sucked in a breath.

"He must be *hot.* What's his name?"

"Elan." Just saying his name made her face flood with heat. Guilt.

"Wow. Is he married?"

"No! Do you really think I would sleep with a married man?" A rush of indignation made her shove her hand through her hair.

"I didn't think you'd sleep with your boss."

Me neither.

"You haven't told him yet, have you?"

"No. You're the first person I've told. He's not going to be happy, and that's an understatement. After it happened he said we should never mention it again."

"You could sue for sexual harassment." Her sister's voice was low, serious.

"I can't. He actually predicted something like this might happen. He didn't want a young female assistant for that very reason and he tried to get me transferred on my first day. I told him that if my behavior was at all unprofessional—" She sucked in a breath. "He could fire me on the spot."

"Oh, Sara." There was a pause. Sara heard her little nephew say something and his mom whispered a quick reply, then came back on the line. "Don't tell him. Seriously, you don't want to lose your medical insurance at a time like this. Trust me on this one. Been there, done that. I don't know what I would have done without Derek helping me out."

"Derek's going to have a cow, isn't he?" Derek, their oldest brother, had been like a second father to her. More of a father than her real one. He'd worked so hard, taking a second job to help the family through one crisis after another. They'd all been blindsided by Erin's unexpected pregnancy followed by their mother's diagnosis with lymphoma. Sara cringed at the thought of dealing him another blow.

"Derek is a rock. He never said a single negative thing when I got pregnant. He's been there for me every step of the way. We'll all support you. Kristin can look after your baby while you work. She'll be able to have her entire in-home daycare be our kids—it'll be fun. I've missed you so much. You are going to move home, aren't you?"

A question that had zinged around her mind from the moment she learned the news. How could she not move home and be with her family?

But then again, how could she?

"There are no jobs in my field there." She looked out the window at the harsh desert landscape, mountain peaks dark against the shimmering sky. So beautiful.

"Bates Electronics will take you back."

"But I won't make enough to pay down Mom's hospital bills.

I know we're all trying to contribute, but my salary is by far the highest. And then there are my college loans. All of you have your own responsibilities to deal with."

"You don't always have to be a superwoman, you know? It's okay to be human."

No, it's not. I made that mistake one night in the desert.

"I don't think Elan will fire me. If he was going to, he'd have done it already. I promised him on my first day that I wouldn't so much as flirt with him. I guess he has women throwing themselves at him all the time, I just can't believe I turned out to be one of them."

"He sounds like a piece of work. I'd like to get my hands on him."

Erin's gritty threat almost made her laugh. "That's how this whole thing got started, I'm afraid." She took a deep breath. "I'm going to tell him about the pregnancy tomorrow."

"Oh, Sara." Her spirited sister's voice withered. "You know Gavin dumped me when I told him."

Sara rubbed her eyes. "I know. I just hope I can be as strong as you."

Okay, this is it. You're going to march right into his office and say it. I'm pregnant.

Sara inhaled a shaky breath as the elevator climbed. She'd deliberately come in late, so he'd be there and she wouldn't have time to sit around at her desk and think of reasons not to tell him. She'd even bicycled here in a smart pantsuit so she'd be "dressed for the occasion." Unfortunately, there was now a black chain print smudged near the inside of the right ankle. She'd deal with that later.

The elevator doors opened, and her anxiety turned to chilling surprise.

Her desk, which had sat right in front of the elevator, was now moved to one side, sharing the space with a second identical desk. The piles of papers covering her workspace threatened to keel over onto the stark gray surface of the new desk pushed up next to it.

"Sara." Elan's large form dominated even the cavernous space of the foyer. His greeting caused her heart to pound louder.

I'm pregnant.

But she couldn't tell him now because there was another person in the room.

"This is Mrs. Dixon," Elan said. A satisfied smile roamed across his mouth. "She's a new member of our team. Her title is Executive Assistant."

Sara's blood froze. Was she being replaced?

"Mrs. Dixon will perform the secretarial duties that were your responsibility. Answering my phone, preparing my correspondence, filing my papers and such."

Sara struggled to keep her face expressionless. *And what will I do?*

"You will focus your time and energy on special projects I assign you. This arrangement is somewhat inconvenient," he indicated the two desks with a sweep of his hand. His gold watch glinted beneath a starched cuff. "But it's temporary. I'd like you to gain more experience in the field, to become familiar with the day-to-day operations at our job sites."

Sara blinked, the lights suddenly too bright for her eyes. She glanced at Mrs. Dixon. Steel-gray hair sprayed into a bouffant, mouth pursed into a prim line, the stiffly suited older woman regarded her with what looked like distaste.

I prefer my executive assistant to be a woman with decades of experience, and preferably gray hairs on her head.

Elan's words on that first day flew into her head.

She was being replaced. And banished. He meant to be rid of her, and since she wouldn't quit he planned to send her away to "gain experience." And he'd installed her replacement before she was even gone.

"Your salary will increase, of course." Elan's words jerked her attention back to him. He surveyed her through narrowed eyes. "Commensurate with your new responsibilities and the inconvenience of frequent travel."

Frequent travel. On a plane. Her gut clenched at the prospect. Is this how he meant to drive her away? To play on her one weakness?

"It is a promotion, though your title will remain the same." An overhead spotlight threw his arrogant features into harsh relief as a smile crossed his lips.

A promotion. Higher pay. A reward for excellence?

Or a smoke screen to cover his plan to force her resignation?

"Thank you. I look forward to the new challenges," she said stiffly.

"Good. I have a meeting to attend. Please familiarize Mrs. Dixon with the workings of our office. I'll be at home this afternoon as I have a new mare being delivered. You may handle my calls for me."

With a brusque nod, he strode toward the elevator leaving Sara alone with…

The Other Woman.

She wanted to laugh. Her rival was not the long-lashed, pouty-lipped casino bunny she might have imagined. No. She was a heavily powdered, sturdy-legged matron of at least fifty-five.

"Pleased to meet you," she said, holding out her hand to Mrs. Dixon.

"Likewise." Mrs. Dixon's hair remained firmly in place as she nodded a greeting and met Sara's sweating palm with her own cool, meaty hand. "Have you worked here long?"

"Nearly five months."

Oh, and I'm having his baby, by the way.

How would she ever tell him now? With this steel-haired battle-ax perched outside the office door, ear probably glued to the intercom?

As hers had once been.

"I have thirty-five years of experience assisting executives." Mrs. Dixon's thin lips pressed together for a moment as she glanced from Sara's travel-wrinkled suit to the teetering piles of folders and correspondence on her desk. "We'll soon get this office whipped into shape."

I have to tell him. Today.

She pumped down on the pedals, pushing her bike along the dusty road that cut through the sagebrush-strewn desert. She pedaled slowly, trying to conserve her energy, trying not to work up too much of a sweat as the summer sun glared down at her from the fierce blue sky. It was already eleven o'clock, the journey taking longer than she'd expected. When she'd looked up Elan's address she hadn't realized his ranch was so far from town. But she had to go there and tell him away from the prying eyes of their coworkers.

She'd tried, time and time again over the past two weeks, to get a moment alone with Elan behind the closed door of his office. But Mrs. Dixon hovered around him like a ministering angel, bearing cups of steaming coffee, bags of dry-cleaned shirts and freshly collated reports. She even took shorthand, which seemed to delight Elan, who now dictated most of his personal correspondence instead of typing it himself on his computer. There was no escaping the woman, whose old-school solicitude was a stark contrast to Sara's own ambitious careerism.

And Elan was using her ambition as a rope to hang her with. She was scheduled to leave next Thursday for three weeks on an offshore rig in the Gulf of Mexico. After that she was headed to Canada, for a long stint at three different sites there. The opportunity was exciting, she couldn't deny it, but it was sure to be a challenge in ways she probably couldn't even imagine. No question, he was pushing her, testing her, trying to find her limits.

He'd wanted her gone, and now she would be. Good. No more struggling to keep her eyes off the broad strength of his shoulders, the dexterous power of his hands, the dark magnetism of his gaze.

What a relief. So why the hollow ache inside her at the thought of leaving?

Probably that hollow space was there because she'd been up half the night drafting projections for a new client, with nothing more than a quick plate of fruit and cheese to keep her going.

She didn't think he'd fire her when he heard her news. She'd been at the company long enough to know that for all his brash demeanor Elan treated his employees with scrupulous fairness. There were several pregnant women in the office and he'd even raised the idea of an on-site daycare to encourage employee retention.

His objections would be *personal*.

If he was trying to force her out now, how would he react when he knew her secret? Even if he didn't fire her, he might push just hard enough to get her on that train home to Wisconsin.

Telling him was risky, but she wasn't the kind of person who could sit on a secret like this. It was his child, too, and he deserved to know of its existence.

She'd reached a flat expanse of land on which she couldn't see a man-made structure of any kind, let alone a house befitting a wealthy tycoon. Was she lost?

She hadn't phoned to tell him she was coming. She'd figured the surprise of her unexpected appearance would only herald the other, far more dramatic surprise that she had in store for him. But if she didn't find the place soon, the surprise would be finding her bleached bones out on the burning sands.

As she came to the top of a slight rise she spied movement off in the distance. Dark lines of pipe fencing crisscrossed the desert, marking boundaries on the open plain. She squinted against the high sun, trying to make out the shadowy shapes that darted to and fro in the distance.

A man and a horse.

A dark horse and a dark-skinned man silhouetted against the sun-bleached landscape. Gradually she saw the shape of the house emerge from its surroundings. Sand-colored, it blended almost totally into the environment. Other horses sheltered in the dark shade of earth-toned structures that became visible as she drew closer.

A trickle of sweat pricked at her spine, and her heart raced as much from fear as from physical exertion as she drew closer to her quarry.

He hadn't seen her.

Elan stood in the center of a round pen. The dark-red horse ran on the end of a long lead, as he chased it around in circles. When the horse slowed or tried to turn away from him, he cracked a whip to drive it forward.

His attention focused totally on the horse, he didn't look up even as she dismounted her bike. She leaned it against the sand-colored wall of the imposing bunkerlike structure that she assumed must be his house.

She approached slowly, her heart thundering against her ribs. The pen Elan worked in stood a good hundred yards away and she struggled to put one foot in front of the other and cover what suddenly seemed like an impossibly large distance.

She couldn't back out this time. Wouldn't leave until she'd told him.

"Yah!"

His shout startled her and she jumped. But he'd shouted at the horse. His expression frightened her, brows low over eyes narrowed against the bright sun, chin jutted in an expression of determination.

Her gaze dropped lower. He wore only a pair of dusty black jeans. His bare torso shone with sweat in the blazing midday heat. His hair was damp, black tendrils plastered to his forehead. He raised a muscled arm and buried his face in the crook of his elbow, streaking a mix of sweat and dirt across his face as he raised his focus again to his horse.

And then he saw her.

The rein to the horse went slack and the animal slowed to a halt. Elan raised his hand higher to shield his eyes from the sun and squinted at her as if doubting his vision.

"Sara?"

Her heart tripped over itself and her breathing quickened as she walked to him on unsteady legs. "Yes."

"What brings you to my home?" Still squinting against the sun, he started to stride toward her. The horse, however, had other ideas and tossed its head, almost jerking the rein from his hand.

Elan jerked back and let fly a string of words in a language she didn't know. "This mare, she has the stubbornness of an ox, the disdain of a camel!"

Sara looked at the mare. She had her head raised and one eye firmly fixed on Elan in an attitude of visibly insolent disregard. "I'm training her to see if she's suitable to breed to my stallions."

"But she has other ideas?" Sara raised an eyebrow. She was relieved by the minor distraction of talking about the horse. An icebreaker, if ice could even be imagined in the blazing heat of the desert.

"Yes. She'd like to train me to leave her alone with her food." Elan's lips curved into a smile. The mare seized the opportunity to turn her backside to him. Elan cracked the whip and goaded her into a swift canter around the pen, then brought her to a halt.

"There's no point in breeding a horse that cannot safely be ridden, no matter how lovely her conformation," he continued, as he gathered up the length of rein and led the horse across the pen to where Sara stood.

"She's beautiful."

"Yes, but beauty without loyalty can break hearts—and

bones." He smiled broadly and patted the horse's neck. "She'll bend to my will. It's only a matter of time. I feed her, I care for her, give her shelter from the sun. She will learn these things come with a price, and she'll learn to pay it."

Sara nodded and looked at the beautiful sorrel mare, who tossed her head constantly, obviously hating the confinement of her halter. Her heart swelled with pity for the creature that wanted to be free, but would have to learn that her days of illusory freedom were over.

She knew that feeling.

At that instant the child stirred inside her, a strange new fluttering sensation that tugged her attention back to her purpose. Her fingers drifted instinctively to the place where her baby was secreted in her belly. Elan's eyes narrowed as they followed the motion, and she yanked the traitorous hand behind her back.

"I need to talk to you." Her gut tightened and her breathing slowed, making her light-headed.

"Yes?"

"Can we…I know you're busy, but can we…go inside?" She couldn't stand there in the heat much longer without keeling over. Her fingers and toes stung with needle pricks of awful anticipation and her heart bumped almost painfully against her ribs.

"Of course." He paused for a moment, regarding her steadily. "I'll put Leila in her paddock." The expression on his face showed that he realized it was a serious matter. Elan was not a man to waste words teasing out the reason for her visit. They walked in silence together as he penned the horse and removed its halter.

The shade of the barn was a merciful relief from the unrelenting heat of the sun. He hung up the halter and lead in a tack room, then glanced down at his dusty, sweaty body.

"Please excuse me a moment." He picked up a hose and turned the spray directly on himself. A few stray drops splashed on Sara and the icy coldness of it startled her.

Rivulets of water streamed over his back and down the taut muscles of his torso as he held the hose above his skin. He bent his head forward and ran the water directly into his hair, ruffling it with his fingers and sighing as the cool liquid touched his scalp.

A rush of heat made Sara cringe as her body responded so predictably to the sight of his impressive physique as he cooled and cleaned his skin with the fresh water.

When he turned the hose off, his jeans were soaked down to midthigh and his upper body glistened with clear droplets. Sara struggled to keep her breathing inaudible as she watched the water drip sensuously over the curves of his thick muscles. Drops traced the deep hollow of his spine down to where his wet jeans hugged his rounded backside.

As he turned, her eyes automatically followed the trails of water that gathered between his pectorals and slid into the line of black hair tracing the distance from his belly button to the fly of his low-slung jeans.

She really was a hopeless case.

"Come this way," he said. Mercifully he didn't look at her long enough to notice the effect of his impromptu shower on her sanity.

He kicked off his boots outside a wide, arched doorway, then pushed open the door and ushered her inside. The thick earthen walls that blended so easily with the desert opened into a softly lit, cavernous space. A fountain trickled steadily in the center of the room, creating a cool and peaceful atmosphere. Subtle earth-toned patterns ornamented the bare walls.

"It's beautiful," breathed Sara, her eyes wide. "Should I take my shoes off?" The space felt like a sanctuary. It was, no doubt, Elan's refuge from the pressures of the business world.

"If you wish."

She slid off her sneakers and her tired feet reveled in the sensation of deliciously cool stone under their soles. Elan strode across the tiled floor toward another arched doorway.

"Come in here." He held a door open. She accidentally brushed against his arm as she moved past him. The drops of water that passed from his skin to hers sizzled as his touch stung her with a surge of electrical energy.

"Please sit and relax. I'll be right back."

Two vast leather sofas flanked a fireplace outlined in pale marble. A wall of windows was shaded from the sun by gauzy pale curtains that moved in the air-conditioned breeze.

She seated herself gingerly on one of the sofas, the leather cool against her skin. The painting above the fireplace looked like a Mark Rothko original, a cool square of blue hovering in a field of gray.

Elan returned wearing a clean pair of jeans and nothing else. Drops of water still glittered on his torso. His uncombed hair fell seductively to his eyes. What did she expect? She'd invaded his home without asking, interrupted his work, did she think he'd put on a suit for her?

He carried two frosted glasses of water. "Here, drink this."

She took it from him, icy drops stinging her fingertips. He sat on the opposite sofa and leaned back, broad bare shoulders sprawled on the dark leather. He took a sip of water and looked at her expectantly.

Silence hung in the air and a surge of panic shot through her as she realized the time had come for her confession. She cleared her throat and placed her glass on the floor with an awkward clunk.

"Er, Elan…" Blood rushed around her brain as she struggled to keep her thoughts coherent. She'd tried rehearsing what to say, but her attempts always dissolved into panicked babbling or tearful self-pity. This was no time for self-pity. She took a deep breath and straightened her spine. "I have something to tell you."

His brow furrowed. She waited for him to interject a polite response, along the lines of "Oh?" or "What is it?" but he didn't.

He merely took another sip of his water and regarded her steadily through hooded eyes.

"I…I don't know how to tell you this…" she paused again and wrapped her arms around herself as if assaulted by a cold gust of wind. Elan's eyes narrowed and he put his glass down. He adjusted the waist of his jeans against his hard, tanned belly and leaned forward a little. Expectant.

The baby shifted, flooding her with resolve.

"I'm pregnant."

He blinked. Other than that he didn't move a muscle. He stared at her, and his eyes searched her face. A furrow appeared above one eyebrow. Sara shrank inside. Did he not believe her?

"I…I…I'm four months along."

His brow creased into a deep frown and his lips parted. His eyes darted down to her belly, which she realized she was clutching, then back up to her face.

Sara struggled to find the words to make it seem real. "I'm going to have a baby."

The words hung in the air for a few seconds as he continued to gaze at her in astonishment. Then he sprang to his feet and strode across the room, bare feet on the stone floor.

He still hadn't uttered a word.

Sara shriveled inwardly and dropped her eyes to the floor as she heard his footfalls moving away from her. She'd tried and failed to imagine what his reaction might be. She'd never seen him fly into a rage at the office. His anger was always quiet and controlled, a fire burning deep within.

Was he angry?

She sneaked a glance across the room, and at that very moment he wheeled around and stared at her. His eyes were blazing, his face set in a stony expression that was unreadable, frightening.

"You've carried this secret for four months?" The words seemed to emerge from a closed mouth, hissed between tight lips.

"I've only known for two weeks," she whispered. Her heart clenched as she saw a shadow of confusion cross his features. He stared at her a few more seconds, then turned abruptly away again. He strode around the perimeter of the large room and approached her until he was standing over her, his shadow invading her space.

"May I see your belly?" His voice emerged low and quiet, yet clearly a demand. His request wasn't polite, but then it wasn't a gracious situation. Sara rose to her feet ungracefully. She knew her face was blazing as she lifted her T-shirt and pushed down the waistband of her bike shorts.

She avoided his eyes and looked down at her belly. It looked so vulnerable, pale and soft, a slight curve that announced the presence of a third person in the room.

Elan slowly lifted his right hand and reached out to her abdomen with his fingers extended. She heard his intake of breath as the tips came to rest on her skin. Gradually, gently, he lowered his hand until it covered her belly, cupping the roundness.

Her womb stirred under his touch. A sudden rush of sensation flooded her limbs. She struggled to keep her breathing under control. Didn't dare look at his face. Her nipples tightened involuntarily and she tore her eyes away, desperate that he not see the way her body responded to the gentle pressure of his hand.

For, even now, Elan's touch made her body hum with thrilling awareness. A dangerous awareness of his hard-sprung masculinity, his harsh beauty. Humbling awareness of the razor-sharp intellect that matched her own. But above all, awareness of the man who had loved her that night with a passion and tenderness that would haunt her as long as she walked the earth.

He pulled his hand back. "We must marry."

The words, spoken low and fast, blew away the fog of sensation that had engulfed her.

"What?" She barely recognized her own voice. It sounded

strangled, distant. With a tremendous effort of will she looked up at his face.

His eyes blazed with black fire. He looked directly at her, his features set in an expression of determination.

"You will be my wife."

She fumbled with her shorts and T-shirt, covering the exposed flesh of her belly. She felt altogether naked and exposed in the face of his authoritarian command.

But she shook her head.

Elan's eyes narrowed, but he didn't speak.

"I can't marry you." Her voice was clear, quiet but resolute.

"Why not?" The words flew from his mouth in a growl.

"Because…"

Because you don't love me.

She couldn't bring herself to say the words. Certainly in her mental anguish she'd imagined the possibility of a proposal. It was, after all, the honorable thing to do. And Elan was an honorable man.

She was "in trouble" and he was the man who'd gotten her that way. Even in the twenty-first century it was still common politeness that he should offer to give the child a name. It was the same reason her father had proposed to her mother, decades ago, when her oldest sister had come unexpectedly into existence.

Elan regarded her with total astonishment. His brow lowered farther as he raised his hands to his hips. "You refuse me?"

Sara swallowed hard. Her hands flew to her belly and clutched each other, fingers trembling. "Yes," she whispered. "I can raise my child alone."

The confusion that darkened his face tore at her heart. For an instant she itched to step toward him, throw her arms around him and shout "Yes, I'll marry you, I'll be your wife and bear all your children and we'll live happily ever after!"

And the thought brought a fresh flush of color to her cheeks.

A twinge of embarrassment that she could harbor such childish fantasies. That she could dream even momentarily of a happy future with a man who'd made it crystal clear that ardent women were the bane of his existence.

No doubt her mother had nurtured those same foolish fantasies when she'd chosen marriage over single motherhood—a miserable marriage that had drained her strength and kept her constantly pregnant or tending to a baby, despite her increasingly poor health. That had kept her chained to a cruel man who cheated on her and to a succession of low-paying part-time jobs that would never give her the means to escape.

Sara didn't intend to make that same mistake.

Eight

Elan tore his eyes off her and strode across the room. His mind whirled with confused thoughts and he couldn't grab a single sensible one from the mix.

Sara is pregnant with my child.

He'd needed to place his hand on her belly to fully accept the truth of it. And nothing could prevent his heart from soaring with the knowledge.

He was assaulted with a vision of Sara living in his home, of the quiet desert ringing with the sounds of childish laughter. For an instant all the entanglements he'd dreaded seemed like the most blissful kind of bondage he could imagine. Sara in his bed each morning. A family to provide and care for the way a man is born to. A son or daughter—and the promise of more—to carry his legacy into the future.

Then she'd refused him.

His gut burned with unfamiliar emotion as he wheeled around

to face her. She looked so small and delicate standing there, clutching her belly with both hands as if he might try to rip the baby right from her womb.

"You wish to deny me the right to raise my child?"

She flinched as he said *my child*. Blinked and looked down at the floor. An ugly thought sneaked up on him, bringing with it a cold chill of fear.

She'd said she was pregnant, but she had not said the baby was his.

Was it possible that she carried another man's child and was merely informing him of her pregnancy as a professional courtesy? The image of Sara with another man assaulted him like a kick in the gut.

"Is it my child?" The words shot from his mouth like bullets from a gun. There was no dignified way to ask the question, but he had to know.

Sara nodded, her face flushing crimson. "Yes," she hissed between closed lips.

Recrimination seized him as he realized how he'd shamed her with his doubt. "I apologize. I didn't mean to imply…" He couldn't bring himself to spell it out. The idea of Sara with another man stole his breath.

Since that one night in the desert he'd been tormented by the longing to gather her in his arms again. He was haunted by memories of her gentle touch, her fiery passion. But the memories were tainted by the realization that he'd taken advantage of her.

She was a young girl, barely out of college. Even if she had desired him, too—at that moment—he should have known better than to let the situation get out of control. Than to let himself get out of control.

He was her boss. The abuse of his authority was inexcusable. When she'd accepted his apology without protest, she confirmed that night had been a terrible lapse of judgment. As he'd suggested, they had never mentioned it again.

Determined to rid himself forever of his craving to hold her, of the memories he couldn't seem to shake, he'd done his best to challenge her beyond her capacity and drive her away.

When that hadn't worked he'd planned to send her away. Push her out of sight, out of reach, out of his mind. To rid himself of the compulsion to take her in his arms, of the foolhardy urge to protect and care for her.

He didn't need her.

But now there was a child to consider. That changed everything.

She regarded him steadily with those cool, pale eyes that haunted his nights. A few strands of golden hair had escaped her bun and curled around her face. She reached up and gathered them in her hands, tucking them back into the knot behind her head.

The movement of raising her arms pulled her T-shirt tight against the new fullness of her belly and the heavier curve of her breasts and he looked away quickly as his breath hitched. Her pregnancy did not dampen his desire for her.

Anger sliced through him. Anger at the power she had over him, power only magnified by the fact that she carried his child.

Power he could harness only though marriage.

Why did she refuse him? It was hard to comprehend. Perhaps she felt guilty for breaking the pact that *she* had proposed on her first day of employment?

They had both broken it. That was moot and it was time to move forward.

"I hold myself fully accountable for this unfortunate situation. You bear no blame—"

"But I—" She began to protest and he held up his hand to silence her.

"Your pledge to me on the first day of employment was broken by my rash actions, not yours. Rest assured, we'll never mention it again. I will provide you and our child with every advantage and opportunity. As my wife, you'll want for nothing. You will bear my name and we'll share life as a family."

Already his heart swelled with the idea. How strange that the universe should provide such an opportunity! That fate should deliver a woman into his arms who was his match in every way.

Their marriage was an ideal outcome to this strange predicament.

"We'll make our announcement tomorrow. We'll be married before the month is out and our child will suffer no shame." He rubbed his hands together. "We shall plan the wedding immediately, perhaps by next week—"

"I can't marry you." She spoke quietly, but with no hesitation. Her renewed refusal struck him like a slap.

"But you must. Can't you see that?" He couldn't keep angry indignation out of his voice.

She looked away across the room for a moment, as if gathering her thoughts, then back at him, eyes wide. "I know that in some ways marriage does seem like the sensible thing, the obvious thing to do, but I also know that in the long run we'd both regret it. We'd feel trapped, like we were forced together."

"Arranged marriages are common in my country. Few matches arise out of love, but many achieve it."

The cruel irony stung him. He was making the argument his father had made to him when he came of age. A suitable bride, a lifetime of duty. He'd rejected it out of hand and claimed the right to choose his own bride, shape his own destiny, even if it meant abandoning his homeland for good. He'd given up enough already at the hands of his father.

"Did your parents have a happy marriage?"

Sara's question penetrated the dark fog of ugly memories that surrounded his last face-to-face encounter with the man who stole his childhood.

"No." He would not lie to her.

She turned to face him, fixed him with her wide-eyed stare. "So you know firsthand that a marriage of convenience doesn't always lead to—love." The last word caught in her throat slightly and Elan's heart constricted as she said it.

Love. It was not a commodity to be bought or sold, searched for, found or extracted with the aid of high-tech equipment. It was something strange, unknowable, elusive—that no amount of money could buy.

He doubted he would know it if he saw it. His life had been empty of love since his mother's death. Even his once-beloved brothers were now virtual strangers to him, all of them victims of his father's power games.

"What went wrong in your parents' marriage?" She asked the question cautiously. He bridled at the unpleasant prospect of airing his family's dirty linen with an outsider. Some things were better left unspoken. But her steady gaze called to him, demanded his honesty.

"My father liked to be in control and to have those around him know he was in control."

"And he tried to control your mother?" The pulse flickering at her throat contradicted her calm voice.

"Yes. She was much younger than he, bright and free-spirited, with her own way of doing things." Elan swallowed. Even after all these years he could still see her smiling face, feel the soft touch of her soothing hands. He'd clung to those memories as a balm to his loneliness. "My father did not brook any contradiction."

"So they argued?"

"Yes. About many things. Until my father declared that in his household he laid down the rules and everyone would obey. When my mother defied him he punished her in the harshest way he could think of. By taking her sons away and sending them abroad."

"Including you." Her eyes narrowed and he stiffened at what looked like pity in her expression.

"Yes. She died shortly afterward and his punishment was inflicted permanently on all of us. He died a lonely and bitter old man who had lost his sons, as well as his wife."

"That's terrible."

The soft expression in her eyes seemed to invite him to sink into the warm comfort of her arms, but her rigid posture held him at bay and those wide jade eyes begged him to keep his distance.

He straightened his shoulders, held his head erect. He didn't need her sympathy or anyone else's. A hard shell had formed around the tender core of his emotions and now he supposed there was nothing left inside it to give or receive love.

His deficiencies must be obvious to Sara. She was a lively young girl who hoped to spend her life with a whole man, not one whose spirit was hollowed by loneliness and toughened by exile.

"If you think it's best, I'll offer my resignation." Her words penetrated his grim thoughts.

"No!" Heat surged through him.

She took a quick step back as if he might hurl himself at her, then quickly steadied herself, one hand resting on her belly.

"You must not leave your job." The thought struck a chord of alarm. That she might get on a train, leave town and never come back... It was not something he could contemplate.

Conviction roared through him. Immediate marriage was the only possible course of action. It was the sensible thing to do. The right thing to do. His heart played no role in his decision. He would handle this situation as he would manage any business crisis, with decisive action.

"You will remain at the headquarters, of course. As for travel in your condition—"

"If I stay I shall continue my job exactly as planned. I do not wish for any special favors or considerations. I'll leave for Louisiana next week as we discussed."

He blew out a snort of laughter. "You can't stay on a drilling rig. It's dangerous and dirty."

"No more so than it was yesterday, when you briefed Mrs. Dixon and myself on my responsibilities there."

"Yesterday, you weren't pregnant." He shoved a hand through his hair. This situation was a challenge to his wits. "Of course, you *were* pregnant, but I didn't know that at the time. It is the nature of our business that it's dangerous and dirty, there's no avoiding those aspects of it, but you will certainly not risk exposure to pollutants while you're pregnant with our child."

"El Mansur Associates prides itself on the containment of potentially harmful substances at all phases of exploration and recovery," she said, her eyes flashing a challenge at him. "One of my tasks is to make sure those goals are being met."

He suppressed a chuckle. Yes, this woman was a match for him. "You will stay at the head office during your pregnancy. I have need of you here."

She lifted her chin. "I would prefer to be in the field," she said coolly.

"As I said, I have need of you here."

She stiffened and her eyes narrowed. "You are *the boss.*"

A cool finger of sensation slid up his spine. He risked abusing his authority again in this situation. Still, the circumstances called for a strong guiding hand.

"I will exert my authority in matters of business. It's a question of liability, surely you understand that?"

She hesitated, drew in a breath. "I understand." She held her chin high, proud and beautiful, her face radiant and her body strong, yet soft and devastatingly female. Her eyes glittered, the flecks of gold catching light from the skylights overhead. Her cheeks were pink from the physical exertion of her long bike ride and the mental exertion of revealing her secret.

And what a secret!

A secret that would change his life forever. Until now he'd wanted nothing more than the quiet calm of solitude. He'd grown weary of eager females and the entanglements they tried to thrust on him.

But despite all his efforts to the contrary, this woman had crept into his mind and cast a spell on him. Now their blood was linked in a child they'd created and there was no way she could leave him now. He'd make sure of it.

Sara was growing light-headed under Elan's steady gaze. Her blood seemed to be draining away, and with growing terror she realized she might actually pass out. She'd been running on adrenaline all morning, and her blood sugar must be getting dangerously low.

"You look pale," his brow lowered in concern.

"I…I'm rather hungry. Would it be possible to—"

"Of course, you must eat. Come with me."

He held out his strong hand and reluctantly she took it. Heat coursed through her as his fingers closed around hers and his thickly muscled arm drew her gently to her feet. He gripped her hand, firm but gentle, as he led her across the cool stone.

As he guided her through the cavernous space of his house, emotions and sensations buzzed in her mind and body like a swarm of bees in a hive. There was massive relief that she'd finally let the proverbial cat out of the bag. She was grateful that he'd taken the news relatively calmly.

But not as calmly as she'd hoped. He wanted his child.

The situation paralleled that of her parents far too closely. She knew her mother had refused her father at first. She'd known he was a ladies' man who didn't love her. But he'd worn her down with his pleas that marriage to her child's father was the "sensible thing" to do.

And in some ways it *was* sensible, at least initially. But in the long run it made for a bitter, hate-filled marriage that cast a pall of misery over their home life and her childhood.

She was fiercely attracted to Elan, but that was just one more reason to guard against him. No doubt he was aware of the power he had over her. To him she was just another of those lecherous women who couldn't keep their eyes and hands off him.

He'd probably expected her to gleefully accept his proposal of marriage and rush into his arms, only to spend the rest of her life wrapped in a cocoon of regret as he grew to despise her more and more for each year he stayed in a marriage that sprang out of circumstance rather than love.

If Elan was anything like her father, he'd feel free to continue the lifestyle he'd pursued before marriage. He'd be out there under the desert moon, burning mesquite with another woman, while she stayed home taking care of the children.

Her heart squeezed at the thought of Elan with another woman. For all she knew, he did have a girlfriend, or a stable of them. She'd rather walk barefoot through the desert in the blazing midday heat than even catch a glimpse of him with someone else. Just one of the many reasons she'd prefer an oil rig on the open sea to a desk outside his office.

"The kitchen. Please, take a seat at the table. I'll find something for you to eat."

He released her hand and she breathed a sigh of relief as cool air replaced his warm grasp.

Commercial appliances gleamed amongst sheets of rare stone. The table she sat at was an extraordinary sliver of metal-flecked granite.

"Would you like some chicken salad?" Elan appeared relaxed and nonchalant as he moved about the large kitchen.

"That would be fine."

He was acting as if nothing had happened. But wasn't that what they did every day at the office? Elan went about the business at hand and she struggled to do her duties while her mind whirled with the torment of wanting to touch him.

And today was no different. The muscles of his powerful back flexed as he pulled open the heavy fridge door, causing an echoing ripple deep inside her. His jeans hugged and molded to the firm curves of his athletic backside and long, sturdy legs.

She drew in a silent breath and prayed to retain at least the appearance of dignity.

He stood in front of the fridge, examining the contents of the neatly stacked crocks inside. She couldn't help but notice his hair was freshly cut, cropped close in back to reveal the thick muscles of his neck.

She started as he turned to her.

"You must be hungry now you're eating for two."

"Er, yes." She was shocked that he could refer so casually to her pregnancy. She still struggled with the reality of it and had to remind herself constantly that she carried another being inside her. Apparently, Elan had no trouble accepting the idea.

He brought out two black ceramic containers and swung the heavy door closed with a denim-clad knee. His bare feet were silent on the stone tile as he moved toward her. Her heart skipped as his eyes met hers.

How could he take this so calmly? Did he really expect her to marry him?

She struggled to plaster a polite expression on her face while her body roiled with the usual mix of uncomfortable sensations that assailed her when Elan was in the room.

His broad hands moved with deft grace as he spooned two salads onto a large black stoneware platter. Even now she was haunted by the sensation of those hands on her, undressing her, roaming over her skin.

Get a grip. It was that kind of thinking that got her in this situation in the first place.

It wasn't fair. They'd used a condom. But she'd discovered to her chagrin that condoms were only about 95 percent effective at preventing pregnancy. She'd fallen into the other five percent.

"My cook is a health nut so you can be sure these salads are packed with nutrients. But I can tell you already take excellent care of yourself." His eyes dropped quickly to her body, then back up to meet hers. Their path left a smoking trail of heat that made her struggle to catch her breath.

She felt underdressed in her tight athletic clothes. She should accept the fact that she was a pregnant woman and start dressing differently. Clinging to her usual attire and habits was a form of denial she couldn't seem to shake.

"I do try to eat healthily. But I haven't gained as much weight as the doctor would like." The confession slipped out as she reached for her fork. She worried that her tendency to deny was somehow depriving her baby.

Concern flashed across his face as his brows lowered. "How much are you supposed to gain?"

"She'd like me to have gained eight to ten pounds by now," she mumbled as she dug her fork into Chinese chicken salad with a mouthwatering aroma of sesame oil. "Because I'm a little underweight."

"And how much have you gained?"

She hesitated. "Only four pounds. But the doctor says the baby's growing fine." She forked the salad into her mouth and chastised herself for telling him.

"You're underweight?" His eyes widened. "Forget these salads, they seemed refreshing for a hot day but you need something heartier."

He wheeled away from her and strode back to the fridge. "You must eat as I do—red meat and plenty of it."

Elan's expression was so serious that she couldn't help but laugh. "No, thanks, I've seen you eat and I don't think I'm up to the task."

He turned to face her and she flushed as she remembered the time they'd eaten together—*that night in the desert.*

They'd eaten food, and then they'd tasted each other.

His lips parted as if the memory assailed him, too. Sara felt her blush darken.

Why did you have to bring up that night?

Elan raked a hand through his hair. He took in an audible breath, "That night—"

"Was a terrible mistake," she burst. "It should never have happened." Tears welled up, gagging her throat.

A moment's indiscretion that had permanent repercussions.

His face darkened and he turned away.

Elan drew in a breath. He had been about to suggest that the night itself was unplanned but that its consequences might be…

Wonderful.

He had to make her see that, too.

"Sara, naturally the situation is unexpected. As I've said, I take full responsibility and I assure you that you will want for nothing."

"I don't want your money," she said quickly.

Elan felt a muscle twitch in his jaw. Money? He'd offered to share his life with her and she thought he meant to simply throw money at her? The insult stung him. "Money will be the very least of your needs," he growled.

"I'd like to continue at my job for as long as possible. And," she looked up at him, her soft eyes pleading, "I'd prefer if people didn't know the child was yours."

His gut muscles clenched at the blow.

"It's just that people at work won't respect me if they know that I…"

Slept with the boss.

His heart constricted unpleasantly. He could indeed imagine the snickering and gossiping around the water coolers if people knew she was pregnant—by him.

Of course, if she married him it would be a different story altogether.

He had to make her see reason.

He stood in front of the refrigerator, watching her as she quietly ate the chicken salad. They could be married this week—tomorrow perhaps? He was unsure of the laws involved—and she could announce her pregnancy and her marriage at the same time.

Mrs. Elan Al Mansur.

He had to admit the name didn't suit her well, with her soft pale hair and wide jade eyes. It sounded heavy, weighed down with the centuries of tradition that lay behind it.

But he knew they could make a marriage work. They were a crack team in business. And between the sheets... Well, there hadn't been any sheets, but his temperature spiked as he recalled the joy of being buried inside Sara.

That night, they'd had the world to themselves. The excitement had been explosive, the satisfaction—total. He had never experienced anything like it.

"Sara, I must press my point."

She looked up at him and he watched her bite her lip, anxious.

"*Why,* exactly, do you refuse my offer of marriage?"

If he knew her reasoning, he could make her see sense. He'd built a reputation as a tough negotiator in business. He was skilled at changing minds.

And to his mind marriage was the only reasonable course of action.

She looked up at him. "You don't love me."

She said the words so softly. She blinked, and again her skin flushed.

She was right, of course. He'd lost the capacity for love, but perhaps with her help he might regain it.

"Love grows within a marriage."

"Sometimes it does, sometimes it doesn't. As you know far too well." She straightened in her chair and her eyes glittered.

He regretted relating his family history, because she was right. His own parents' marriage had grown out of tradition and dissolved into disaster. He raked a hand through his hair as if the motion could dislodge sensible thoughts from his brain, but none were forthcoming.

"I like you, Sara. I respect you." His words seemed to come from miles away as they echoed off the stone surfaces in the room.

She looked down at the table and he watched a tear fall and splash on the granite surface as her eyes squeezed shut.

His breath caught in his throat and his hands clenched into fists at the sight.

"Sara, please…" Instinctively he strode toward her, no longer able to resist the powerful urge to take her in his arms. But as he watched, she stiffened. Her eyes sprang open to meet his, shining with tears, begging him to keep his distance.

"No one can predict the future, Elan." Her voice trembled, but she cleared her throat and her next words rang across the kitchen. "My parents married because my mother was pregnant. It proved to be an empty marriage that diminished both of them. I don't want that for myself or my child."

His chest tightened. Her harsh experience echoed his own. His arms still itched to hold her, to close around the slim shoulders she held so rigid.

But now wasn't the time.

Her fiery and stubborn nature demanded skillful handling, much like his new mare. He would take matters into his own hands for now.

Soon, she would be his.

"I'd like to go home now," she said softly.

"Of course."

As Elan sat behind the wheel of his car and watched Sara disappear through the doors of her apartment building, wheeling that infernal bike he'd just taken down from the roof rack, every atom of his being rebelled against letting her go, even for a few hours.

Tomorrow he was ordering her a car whether she liked it or not.

Their wedding would be simple and quiet, yet he would not stint on the luxuries a new bride deserved. Fine gems to bring out the sparkle in her eyes, a lavish gown to complement her lovely figure, gifts to make her laugh with delight.

I'd better get busy.

Nine

Sara stiffened as Elan rested his elbow on the desk, next to the dish of broccoli drenched in fragrant sesame oil, and dangled the keys from one broad finger.

He'd insisted that she join him behind the closed door of his office for a lavish lunch prepared and delivered by his personal chef.

Again he pressed her to accept the new Mercedes E500 he'd ordered without consulting her.

"No, I can't take it." She wiped her fingers on her napkin and sat back in her chair.

"It is a question of efficiency. Your time is better spent working than cycling."

Anger rushed through her. "I don't cycle on company time. I do it on my own time. Am I not always the first person here in the morning and the last to leave in the evening?"

He surveyed her in silence for a moment.

"Your doctor should counsel you not to ride that accursed thing while you're pregnant. Surely the exertion is too taxing on your body?"

"She says that as long as I don't feel overtired or breathless, I can continue all my normal activities. In fact, she told me exercise can make pregnancy and delivery easier."

"Bah. What do doctors know? Driving an air-conditioned sedan is far healthier—and the other drivers can see you coming." He raised an eyebrow as if defying her to deny it.

"I can't accept it." She crossed her arms.

She didn't want to feel beholden to him. She needed to make decisions based on what she truly felt was right, not because she owed anyone a debt of gratitude.

Elan leaned back in his chair and crossed his arms, mirroring her gesture. "There is no arguing with the fact that your cycling keeps you magnificently fit."

His eyes dropped momentarily to her significantly enlarged bust and a smile sneaked across his sensual mouth. She bristled as her nipples stung with awareness of his admiring gaze.

Damn him.

This was a new tactic. Since her announcement three days earlier, he'd taken to deliberately flirting with her. Actively trying to seduce her.

Instead of stiffly holding a door open as she passed through it, he settled his fingers delicately in the small of her back to guide her through. Rather than regard her with measured glances, he now allowed his eyes to linger on her, to drift across her face, hover over her neck and jawline, and occasionally plunge to the swell of her excruciatingly sensitive breasts.

Appreciation of what he saw darkened his eyes, and he did not hesitate to let her see it.

Always struggling with her attraction to Elan, Sara was becoming thoroughly unhinged by his behavior. She knew she should be rankling under the open sexuality of his gaze, bristling with thoughts of sexual harassment lawsuits.

But of course she wanted nothing more than to take him up on his unspoken offer to rip off her clothes and ravish her right there on the carpeted floor of his office.

This new strategy was very, very dangerous.

She pushed her plate of beef teriyaki aside and picked up the drilling proposal they were drafting for a new client.

"Item three, depth of well. It has been determined that the well depth must be no less than thirty-five hundred feet," she said crisply. "That's deep. It'll be expensive."

He paused, looked at her steadily. "Yes, but the rewards promise to be magnificent." He cocked his head and narrowed his eyes slightly. His voice dropped. "Once we establish *steady flow.*"

Perfectly ordinary terminology, said over a perfectly ordinary desk in a perfectly ordinary office. But nothing between her and Elan was ever ordinary, and his husky voice had its intended effect. All sorts of things began to flow inside her—heat, crazy thoughts and warm fluids.

She straightened in her chair. "Indeed," she said, narrowing her eyes. "Is this light, sweet, *crude* we're talking about?"

Elan raised an eyebrow, his full lips curving into a smile.

A treacherous smile threatened to rip across her own mouth.

At that moment the door flung open and Sara jumped in her seat.

Mrs. Dixon's stiff bouffant hair appeared in the gap. "Excuse the interruption, Mr. Al Mansur, I have an urgent phone call for you from Mr. Redding."

"Let me get these dishes out of here." Sara rose and gathered the plates, glad of an excuse to end a conversation that was heading into dangerous territory.

This morning, while his mouth had spoken of soil composition and rock density, his glances had assaulted her with a thousand unspoken words.

Part of her wanted to hear those words—craved them, even—but at the same time she was afraid.

Elan didn't love her. He wanted to marry her for all the wrong reasons.

He was a strong man in every way, his impressive physique only mirrored his fierce determination. She had to make sure she kept her perspective and her distance, and didn't allow herself to be swept away by the sheer force of his will—or by the thrall of desire that still held her captive.

"Let me take those from you, dear." Mrs. Dixon rose to her feet as Sara emerged with the dishes.

"That's okay. I'll just carry them down to the kitchen and put them in the dishwasher."

"Here, let me at least take the plates." She lifted the dirty plates from on top of the stack of serving dishes and pressed the button on the elevator. "Do me good to stretch my legs anyway. Can't have the varicose veins getting the upper hand, now, can we?"

She smiled and Sara smiled back. Despite her formidable exterior Mrs. Dixon was proving to be a nice woman. Helpful to a fault, in a way that made Sara feel selfish and self-important in her hunger for experience and advancement. She hadn't had time to water Elan's plants lately.

They stepped into the elevator.

"Mrs. Dixon, I know you've been doing this type of work for years, and I'm pretty new to it. How do you draw the line between the kinds of tasks you will and won't do?"

"Line? There's no line. I'm employed to keep my executive happy, and I'll do everything within my power to fulfill his needs."

"That sounds rather dangerous!" Sara laughed. "What's the most outrageous thing your boss has ever asked you to do?"

Lie naked beneath him on the desert floor? What on earth

would the prim Mrs. Dixon think if she knew? If she learned that Elan's baby was growing inside her, right now?

"Well." Mrs. Dixon pursed her lips for a moment. Color rose in her powdered cheeks. "I'm afraid that it sometimes falls to me to procure gifts and arrange favors for…how shall I put it?" She tilted her head. "For their mistresses."

"Goodness, do they all cheat on their wives?" The back of Sara's neck prickled.

"Not all of them." Mrs. Dixon pressed her lips together. "But we must remember that these powerful men handle problems and crises that would break an ordinary man. They must have some outlet for their stress." She blinked rapidly.

"I'd certainly draw the line there. There's no way I'd run errands for my boss's bit on the side." The prickling sensation had descended down Sara's arms, causing goose bumps to form.

"Perhaps that's why women of my generation are still in demand." An ice-blue gaze accompanied Mrs. Dixon's tight smile.

Sara blinked. The prickling crept to her fingertips.

"Men have their needs, dear. It's best to accept that." She leaned into Sara with a conspiratorial whisper. "In fact, just this morning Mr. Al Mansur had me arrange insurance and shipping for some gems for one of his ladies."

"What?" Sara spoke too loudly. She'd rattled the plates.

"Yes." They walked into the small galley kitchen and put the dishes on the countertop. "You should see them. Exquisite. Ordered from Mappin & Webb in London. He even showed me some images on the computer and asked for my opinion." She placed her hand on Sara's arm. "Sixty thousand dollars," she whispered. "Whoever gets those will be a very lucky girl."

Spots danced before Sara's eyes as she pulled her arm back and she slid a plate into the dishwasher. A girlfriend? She struggled to keep her breathing inaudible.

Or are they for me?

They hadn't spoken again about his demand that she be his wife. He appeared to have lost interest in the issue for now, which was both reassuring and unsettling at the same time. Did he plan to ply her with gems, as well as heated glances and eighty-thousand-dollar cars? To try and buy her as he'd purchase an expensive new mare?

"Yes, a very lucky girl. They're being delivered to an address on the Vegas strip."

The words hit her like a blow to the solar plexus. Vegas? That was hundreds of miles away.

What a joke that she'd thought they were for her. As if anyone would buy her sixty thousand dollars worth of jewels. The idea was laughable. She gritted her teeth. Would she never learn?

Mrs. Dixon chuckled. "I know you probably find it hard to picture our Mr. Al Mansur with a showgirl, but I've been around long enough to know that even the most serious and business-minded gentlemen enjoy the company of those gay young girls. And why shouldn't he have a beautiful girlfriend, or ten of them? He's not married, after all."

No. He's not married.

The thought of Elan with another woman chilled her. Did he truly plan to marry her, and keep another woman—or women—on the side?

Just like her father.

"Are you all right, dear? You look a bit peaky."

"I'm fine," she rasped. "A touch of indigestion."

"Well, we'd best be getting back to our desks. We don't want Mr. Al Mansur to come out of his office and find we've both gone on the lam, now, do we?"

"No." Sara stumbled behind Mrs. Dixon.

She was *very, very* glad she'd turned down that car. If Elan thought he could buy her for his stable of women, he was very much mistaken.

* * *

The intercom light flared on Sara's phone. What did he want now? She was just getting ready to go home. He'd been calling her into his office all day on one pretext or other and her nerves were in tatters. What she needed right now was to be as far away from him as possible.

"Yes?"

"Please come in."

"I'll be right there." She gathered herself together, tucking a stray strand of hair into her bun.

"Close the door." Elan lounged in his chair, hands behind his head, elbows in the air, broad chest flexed beneath his white shirt.

She closed the door behind her. The baby fluttered in her stomach.

"Congratulations." He smiled enigmatically for a moment. "You won us the Anderson account. They found your presentation and your proposal *very* impressive."

Yes! She narrowly resisted the urge to pump her fist in the air. "Excellent."

"*Excellent* is the only word to describe your performance of late. Though sadly, as a result, my plants are wilting from lack of your tender care and attention. Mrs. Dixon doesn't seem to share your green thumb." His mouth tilted into a smile.

Or your appetite for seduction. He didn't say it aloud, but his stare, heavy-lidded and lingering, conjured the words in the air.

Already her body had started to respond to the unspoken suggestion. She cleared her throat. "I have had my hands full with important projects, as you know."

"Exactly. And, under the circumstances, I intend to lighten your workload considerably." He leaned forward and planted his elbows on the desk. "You should be getting a good night's sleep, conserving your energy, eating carefully prepared, nutritious meals. I'll delegate the Farouk proposal to Andrew, Claire and

Patrick will work on the MacDormand project and I shall take over the Anderson project myself."

A seeping sensation of relief grew into alarm as he spoke. "But that leaves me with—"

"Time to relax and enjoy your pregnancy. You've looked tired lately, and, as you've admitted, your weight gain is not adequate. We must ensure that our baby has every advantage, don't you agree?"

"Well, yes, but…" He was taking away *all* her projects? And he'd already delegated her administrative duties to Mrs. Dixon. Did he intend her to sit in a chair filing her nails all day? Or to spend her time watering his plants?

Or tending to other needs.

Needs that might be better met by an experienced Vegas showgirl.

She clenched her fists. "I'd like to finish calculating the projections for the Farouk proposal myself. I've done a good deal of research and I feel that at this point I can offer the most detailed and comprehensive—" her voice was rising.

Elan silenced her by holding up his hand. "As you wish. Abdul Farouk told me himself how impressed he was by your insight into the complexities of the situation. But be sure to update Andrew on all aspects of the project." He leaned forward and subjected her to another blood-heating stare. "Because imminently I will have another, *very important* project for you."

He held her gaze and she struggled to keep still. To keep her face expressionless as her synapses crackled with a mix of anger and arousal. How did he do this to her?

"I'd better get going," she hissed. "I have a doctor's appointment first thing in the morning. It should be done by nine-thirty so I'll be here before the implementations meeting. I'll have the Farouk proposal on your desk by noon."

"I'm sure you will." A half smile lingered on his full lips. "I have *absolute* faith in you."

The dark rumble of his voice echoed in her ears as she hurried out of the office. Why did it sound as though he meant so much more than her ability to complete an assignment on time? What was he up to?

As she nudged up her kickstand in the parking lot, she looked wistfully at the gleaming silver sedan parked right next to Elan's identical black one. For a moment she allowed herself to feel sad that she couldn't accept it. That she couldn't accept Elan's offer to make her his wife. When her thoughts sneaked off in that direction, the idea of spending her life with him made her spirit soar for a brief, blissful moment.

Until she remembered her mother's stern warnings: "Don't marry a man who doesn't love you. You'll live to regret it. I know I did."

Those words always chilled the heat of her fevered imaginings and brought her back to earth. An earth where she was determined to be dependent on and beholden to no one but herself.

Elan checked his watch. Again. Where was Sara? Her doctor's appointment was supposed to be over by 9:30 a.m. He strode to the window and scanned the parking lot for signs of that accursed bicycle she was so attached to.

A broad smile spread across his face as he saw her turn into the parking lot. A chuckle rose in his throat. She was so graceful, wonderfully athletic, and she carried herself with the dignity of a queen. A queen in Spandex shorts and a sporty maternity top. At least he'd convinced her to start wearing a helmet.

A pleasant warm sensation eased his limbs as he watched her raise herself up to glide over the speed bumps. She made her last turn and headed toward the bike rack that never held more than one bike.

A gray sedan jerked out and sent her sprawling to the hard asphalt.

Yaha!

Terror gripped him and fired every neuron in his body. He grabbed the phone off his desk, shoved out of his office and hurled himself down the stairs, dialing 911 as he ran.

"What is your emergency?"

"Ambulance! She's been hit!"

"Sorry, sir, can you slow down please."

"Sara's been hit by a car.... On her bike." His breathing labored, he pushed out of the emergency exit into the blinding sun of the parking lot. "Five hundred Canyon Road. Please hurry!"

His blood froze as he saw Sara limp and lifeless on the asphalt, the driver of the car standing over her.

He sprinted across the lot and dropped to his knees beside her. He pressed his fingers gently to her neck. Her pulse thumped steadily.

"I didn't see her," said the driver plaintively. Elan ignored him. Sara lay in an awkward position, her eyes closed. But she was breathing.

He fought an overwhelming urge to gather her in his arms. He knew she needed to remain still in case there were internal injuries. He stroked the soft skin of her cheek and heard his own breathing emerge in ragged gasps. He wanted to shout at the ambulance to hurry up, but he didn't want to frighten her in case she could hear him.

Could she hear him?

"Sara?"

No answer, not a flicker of her pale lashes. A fist of fear clenched his heart and he cursed under his breath.

He'd forgotten the phone for a moment, but he pressed it to his ear. "Where is the ambulance?"

"It's on its way, sir. Is the victim conscious?"

"No." He gulped air as his body pounded with adrenaline. "She is not conscious. Hurry! She's pregnant."

"Is her airway clear?"

"Yes, she's breathing."

"Don't move her. The ambulance should be there within five minutes."

The minutes ticked by with agonizing slowness while he held her hand and watched her chest rise and fall silently. Her arms and legs sprawled haphazardly on the hot pavement. He'd never felt so helpless and he burned with the need to do something, anything, he could to help her.

"Sara, can you hear me?"

No answer.

A crowd had gathered around him and he shouted at them to divert the traffic and guide the ambulance in.

Her body looked so small and frail lying there on the ground, the hot desert sun pounding down on her. He wanted to shield her from the harsh rays, to cool the burning asphalt that supported her limp form.

"Sara," he whispered.

No answer.

At last the ambulance roared into the parking lot, siren screaming. The crowd parted as the EMTs unloaded the stretcher, took Sara's vital signs and loaded her onto it.

Elan made a nuisance of himself, begging them to be careful, his gut churning at the sight of her being poked, prodded and hauled into a truck by strangers.

"Stand back!" shouted the EMT, as they prepared to close the doors.

"Let me in!" cried Elan.

"Sorry, sir, no room."

"But she's my...I'm her...I'm the father of her child!" His shout tore through the voices buzzing in the air.

"I'm sorry, sir, we're taking her to General. You can follow the ambulance."

Rage and desperation roared through him as the ambulance doors closed and it ground slowly out of the parking lot. As the vehicle merged back into the highway traffic and its siren turned on, he cursed the skies—his car keys!

He pushed through the crowd of gawking onlookers and shoved back into the building. Ignoring the elevator, he pelted up the stairs, crashed into his office and snatched the keys off the desk. He was sweating and panting by the time he finally got behind the searing-hot wheel of his car and started the ignition.

"Do not let her die!" His angry shout gave no relief.

He blasted the horn hard as a group of pedestrians crossed the road, chatting and laughing. They scowled at him and he banged his hand helplessly on the dashboard. He blamed himself for her accident. How could he have been so negligent as to let her keep riding that ridiculous bicycle in her condition?

From now on he would make sure he took good care of her, whether she liked it or not. It was his duty and he wasn't going to fail again.

He screeched into the parking lot at General and parked directly in front of the emergency room entrance. He abandoned the car with the keys in the ignition and pushed his way through the glass doors into the stark white lobby.

"Sara Daly, where is she?" he demanded of the receptionist, interrupting her conversation with a woman in front of him.

"One moment, please, sir."

"She just came in—she's badly hurt!" He tore away from the desk and moved toward the double doors behind the desk.

"No, sir, you can't go back there!"

"But I need to—" Two orderlies sprang forward and grabbed his arms to restrain him as he attempted to shove his way past the desk. "You don't understand—I'm her…"

Her what? He wasn't her husband, he wasn't even her boyfriend. He was her boss.

"Sir, if you'll please come this way." He'd stopped fighting against the orderlies and allowed them to lead him to a different desk and deposit him unceremoniously in a chair.

"Sara Daly," he said to the silver-haired woman at the glowing computer screen. "I need to be with her," Elan added with force.

"I understand, sir. Let me check her records." She flashed him a kindly glance before turning her attention to her computer screen. "She's been taken into an examination room, the doctor is with her now."

Elan's chest tightened and his fists balled at the thought of Sara laid out on a hard table with a stranger's hands upon her.

"You'll have to wait out here until the doctor—"

"I can't!" He sprang to his feet and instantly the orderlies were at his side again, hands gripping him.

"I know it's a difficult time, sir, but you don't want to distract the doctors and nurses from doing their job."

"No, of course not." He glanced at the orderly to his right and the man shrugged and shot him an expression of sympathy. "I'll wait."

He paced back and forth in the waiting room. This predicament was entirely his fault. He'd broken all his own rules and gotten into a situation where he no longer had complete control. Sara *had* to live. She *must*. And when she did, he'd make sure that they could never be torn apart again.

Sara glanced around the small "room" where the nurse had left her sitting on a wheeled bed. Only a blue curtain separated her from the hallway and the other curtained cubicles. She could hear the patient opposite her speaking to someone in Spanish.

Her ankle throbbed painfully and she half wished she'd accepted the painkillers they'd offered, but the reassuring sight of the slight curve to her belly made her glad she hadn't.

She had no idea how long she'd been in the hospital, though she'd regained consciousness in the ambulance. It seemed an eternity of strangers shining lights in her eyes, attaching electrodes to her belly, kneading and binding her injured ankle. Fear had faded into exhaustion and she couldn't wait to get home.

The curtain twitched aside and Elan entered, eyes fixed on hers. He strode up to her and snatched her hand from her lap.

"Sara." His voice was rough.

"I'm okay, just a badly sprained ankle," she said with forced bravado. "And the baby's kicking like a karate expert."

Elan pressed his lips to her hand and she felt a shudder of warmth reverberate through her bruised and aching limbs. She had a sudden urge to throw her arms around him and hug him, but her battered body and her cautious mind prevented her.

"It's a miracle you weren't seriously injured. In an accident like that, *anything* could have happened." His low voice quivered through her sore muscles. The intensity of his expression threatened to unleash the tangle of emotions she'd been suppressing since she'd awakened—with light blasting in her eyes and strange voices buzzing in her ears—and threatened her calm demeanor.

"I ache all over," she admitted. And she wasn't really talking about her ankle. That hurt, sure, but all of her ached for the love and comfort of someone who cared about her.

Just as the temptation to reach out and hold him became overwhelming, his face hardened. "We must get you home."

"I think the nurse is bringing my discharge papers any minute. The doctor initially wanted to keep me overnight because I lost consciousness. But since the baby is moving well and my vital signs were all good, he agreed to let me go."

"Excellent." Elan clapped his hands together. "Where's that nurse?" He tugged the curtain back and scanned the hallway. "You're coming home with me, by the way. Don't even think of arguing."

"On the contrary, I'd be very grateful if you'd drive me home."

He turned back, a dark eyebrow raised. "When I said 'home with me' I meant home to my house."

"Oh, no. No, I couldn't."

"Did I ask you?" He ducked out of the curtained area in search of the nurse.

Sara tried to struggle to her feet but her right ankle screamed with agony as she put weight on it, and she was unable to suppress a gasp that emerged with a slight shriek.

Elan instantly appeared back in the room. "What happened?"

"I tried to stand," she said sheepishly.

Exasperation twisted his mouth. "Don't compound your injury. There's no need for standing. I'll carry you about in my arms if necessary." His deadly serious tone and demeanor made Sara want to chuckle. She was assailed by an image of him bearing her around belly outward, like an enormous china Buddha.

"I really, really want to go back to my place." She needed to collapse in her own bed and sleep.

"Impossible." He didn't even turn to face her. Sara bridled with indignation. He might be her boss but he couldn't order her around outside the office.

"You have no right!" Her voice sounded shrill.

"Possibly not, but I have two good legs and strong arms, which is more than you can say right now. Where is that damned nurse? I'll carry you out of here right now if I have to." He craned his neck outside the curtains. "Nurse!"

The nurse entered, carrying a clipboard. "I have your release here, if you'll just sign down at the bottom." She handed the clipboard to Sara.

"Sara sustained a blow to the head," said Elan, "there is still a risk of concussion, correct?"

"Yes, she was knocked unconscious. There's no swelling, but—"

"So it's important for her to be with a friend who can care for her and drive her here immediately if symptoms of concussion appear?"

"Absolutely."

Elan assured the nurse she'd be in excellent hands. He went so far as to hold out the hands for examination and the nurse smilingly agreed that she'd never seen a more capable pair.

His expression of smug satisfaction made Sara's hackles rise higher with each second. The tender affection she'd *almost* felt for him a few minutes ago evaporated entirely in the heat of her anger.

She was sure this insistence on taking her to his house tied in somehow with his campaign to get her to marry him—whether she wanted to or not.

As Elan pushed her down the hallway in a wheelchair that he and the nurse had insisted on, she could almost feel the blazing heat of his grin irritating the back of her head.

"Relax, Sara, tension will only slow the healing process." She could hear the smile in his voice and it made bile rise in her gut.

She gritted her teeth. She certainly didn't want anything to slow the process of getting her out of Elan's *capable hands,* and back into the peace and privacy of her own apartment.

If he thought this kind of behavior was going to convince her to marry him, he could not be more wrong.

Ten

"I have a confession to make, Sara."

She was comfortably propped up on pillows in his cozy den, snacks and juice within reach, a thick stack of good books and the TV remote by her hand. Elan enjoyed a surge of satisfaction at seeing her so well settled.

"What?" She lifted an eyebrow and fixed him with a steely stare.

"I may have inadvertently announced the paternity of your baby."

Her head kicked back slightly, but she didn't speak.

He raked his fingers through his hair. "There were a lot of people in the parking lot when the ambulance arrived." He held her gaze. "I may have said something along the lines of 'She's having my baby.'"

He settled his hands on his hips.

Sara's mouth dropped open, then snapped shut.

He shrugged. "They had to find out sooner or later."

She turned her face toward her knees and he watched her shoulders tense.

"They were taking you away, and they wouldn't let me in the ambulance. To be honest, I'm not quite sure what I said. I know I wanted to say 'She's my wife.'"

Her eyes flicked up at him for a split second, then darted back to her knees.

"But since you've not accepted my proposal—*yet*—I merely stated the truth."

His heart quietly thrilled at the knowledge that their secret was out. Such a powerful truth was not a force for good if it remained hidden. Secrets bred secrets, festering into lies, half truths, ugly shadows that warped reality.

"Did they let you in?" She didn't look at him, but the question was not asked unkindly.

"No, but it's no matter. I came anyway."

"I'm sorry they wouldn't let you in the ambulance." She studied her legs—one of them strapped in a black elastic bandage. The other leg looked so delicate beside it, long, slender, suntanned, her bare foot resting on a soft pillow.

She glanced across the room, avoiding him, her pretty brow lined with consternation. "I guess they had to find out eventually." She lifted a slim eyebrow, "I bet they're pretty surprised."

"Their thoughts are no concern of mine."

"I guess I'll just have to get used to it." Her face softened a little, and his own posture relaxed as an odd surge of joy warmed him.

"Does your ankle hurt?"

"A little."

"Can I get you anything?"

She pressed her finger to her lips for an instant, pondering. "Yeah, the moon on a string."

He raised his eyebrows. "Is that some kind of candy?"

"It's a joke." She looked at him, eyes narrowed, mouth utterly unsmiling. "I'm cosseted here with every convenience known to man. I don't think there is anything else I could possibly need. Except the liberty to return to my *own* home."

Her eyes snapped away from him and she tugged at the hem of the boxer shorts he'd lent her. They swam on her charmingly, as did the extra-large T-shirt he'd given her. It was odd how two people who fit together so perfectly could be such completely different sizes.

"I can hear you grinning," she murmured, between gritted teeth.

"The smile is officially wiped from my face." He dragged a hand dramatically over his mouth. The smile, however, was reluctant to depart. While he did not like keeping her prisoner, he certainly did like having her safely within reach.

He did not wish Sara to suffer pain, but he didn't want that ankle to heal any faster than it had to. Settled comfortably in his home, enjoying his tender care, she was sure to see that partnership with him was a welcome, even joyous outcome to the events taking place inside her lovely body.

So everyone knew she'd slept with the boss. Embarrassing, but there it was. The truth. So much for her carefully cultivated air of cool professionalism. That was blown high on the four winds like everything else in her life right now.

And she was going stark, staring, eyes-popping-out, ranting and raving crazy. Elan hovered around her like a giant genie tethered over his bottle, demanding to know her wishes. Didn't he have a company to run?

The sight of him in a crisply tailored suit was enough to send her to the land of gaga. The big, hunky, warm, masculine presence of him dressed in nothing more than a pair of faded jeans threatened to make her beg for mercy.

She knew he was doing it on purpose. He wanted to make sure she saw every tiny ripple that might occur amongst the hundreds of perfectly toned muscles that covered his towering and agonizingly fit physique.

It was cruel and inhumane torture.

It wasn't bad enough that she had a pounding ankle and a bruised butt. No, he had to make sure that her insides pulsed and quivered and simmered uncomfortably in all sorts of inconvenient places. That her nipples were constantly erect and straining against the soft cotton of her borrowed T-shirt. That she couldn't possibly focus on any of the magazines or books or videos he plied her with.

Because she couldn't get her mind off him.

What a jerk.

And he was being so nice. Tending to her needs day and night, arranging the room for her comfort, bringing her favorite foods and an endless stream of hot and cold drinks, fluffing her pillows. Wanting to make her his wife.

It was enough to make a woman lose her resolve. Enough to make her forget about the outside world and cozy up here for good on the Isle of the Lotus Eaters. Enough to make all her plans and dreams and goals evaporate in the face of a plate of handmade bonbons served by a broad hand.

Almost.

"Would you like a massage?" He'd materialized again, heavily muscled arms crossed genie-style, a cheerful smile playing infuriatingly across his bold features.

"No, I would not like a massage!" Her shouted words surprised them both. "Gosh, sorry. I guess being cooped up like this has me wound up."

A mischievous gleam shone in his eyes. "Would you take care of me if I lay injured?" He cocked his head to one side.

"No way. I'd have left you rotting by the roadside." She snapped open a magazine.

"I don't believe you."

"No?" She looked up, an eyebrow raised, daring him to argue

with her. "If I was Florence Nightingale, I'd have majored in nursing, not business management."

"Then perhaps it's lucky our children will have me to tend their wounds." His mouth curved into a crooked smile that made pinpricks of—annoyance, surely?—come alive all over her skin.

"Our children?" Her voice was strangled with fury. "I'm having *one* baby. I've seen an ultrasound. There's only one in there."

"For now." He smiled enigmatically. "I think a massage is definitely in order. You seem very tense." His voice was soft, low, and she could swear for a second that he licked his lips.

Before she had a chance to protest, he'd sprung up onto the chaise behind her and lifted her hair off her neck. He placed his large thumbs on either side of her spine and pushed them, gently but firmly, into the knotted muscle.

"Ohhh!" she cried out with a mix of pain and relief.

"You are in need of *deep tissue* massage," he growled softly, his breath hot on her ear. "*Very* deep."

She whimpered as his callused thumbs found a whorl of painful tension. His masculine scent wound around her, assaulting her senses with a dangerous blend of soap, horse and musky male. Maybe even a dash of crude oil in there to spice the mix. Why did he smell so damn good?

She groaned as his thumbs trailed down her spine, moving in circles that teased pain from deep within. His hot breath tickled the back of her neck as his lips hovered above her skin.

"I have another confession to make," he murmured, his words vibrating off her skin.

Sara gulped. Was he going to confess to his affairs?

I don't want to hear it.

"I must apologize for the way I challenged you with such a demanding workload." His thumbs pressed deep into the tight muscle above her waist. "It was inexcusable."

"On the contrary," she could hardly get the words out as his forceful touch relieved weeks of built-up tension. "I'm grateful for the opportunity to prove myself. Not many bosses would have offered such an opportunity."

Elan chuckled, a low, dangerous sound that echoed deep in her belly. "I don't think *any* would. I confess, my intentions were not entirely honorable."

She froze.

His thumbs stilled. "I meant to push you to your limits, to make you regret the day you met me."

I knew it. Anger sparked inside her, crackled through her muscles.

"Little did I know…" his hot breath tickled the hairs on the back of her neck, "that you would rise so brilliantly to every challenge. Instead, I managed to prove that—without a doubt—you are the only woman for me."

As his words shivered through her like a streak of lightning and sparked a flash of pride, his lips touched the base of her neck. She felt teeth, tongue and then a sensation of being devoured whole crept over her as his fingers roved around her waist and seized her from behind.

A low moan escaped her lips.

Alarm bells sounded in her head. "Wait—"

"You don't mean that." His teeth grazed her neck as his words sank into her consciousness.

He was right. She had no power to resist as his hands moved over her skin, teasing and chafing the surface as his breathing quickened in her ear.

"You are my destiny, Sara. The one woman chosen by the universe to be my bride. I was too stubborn to see that—too blind—until the hand of fate placed my child in your belly and made it clear that we *must* be man and wife."

Sara shuddered as his words struck to her core. Why did it sound so obvious—*so right?*

A swift movement of his powerful legs had him sitting on the chaise in front of her, his handsome face inches from her own. His lids lowered, he picked up the hem of her T-shirt and lifted it. "I want to feel your skin against mine."

His demand rippled through her as he pulled the cotton T-shirt over her head before she could conjure so much as a whimper of protest. Now she wore only shorts and a white sports bra. His big hands settled around her waist and pulled her to him, just as he'd done that night in the desert.

"My Sara." His possessive claim both alarmed and thrilled her, quickening her arousal as his thumb grazed her nipple. Her breathing came faster as his hard-edged cheekbones and aristocratic nose crowded her vision. For a single agonizing second his lips hovered a mere atom's length away from hers. She could feel the heat of his skin, inhale the spicy maleness of his scent. For that single second she thought she might just die if he didn't kiss her *right now*.

Then his lips closed over hers and swept her away in a windstorm of emotion.

She'd never met a man like this. Dangerous in his power, fierce with passion, yet tender in his deft touch. A man of strong emotions buried deep by a lifetime of trial and triumph.

The way he'd reached out to console her during her terror on the plane showed the kind and caring spirit hidden by his stern facade.

Now, as his groan filled her mouth, she knew his bullying insistence on keeping her his prisoner here was driven by his desire to protect her. To keep her safe.

With his powerful arms wrapped around her, her whole body claiming her, she wanted him to keep her safe—forever.

I love you.

She felt the words rising up from deep inside her. Elan kissed her lips repeatedly, licking and teasing them apart until the words felt ready to fall out.

But something still kept them bottled inside her.

She tunneled her fingers into his thick hair, pulled him to her as her body hummed and quivered with maddening arousal.

Why couldn't she tell him? Why couldn't she let him know her feelings for him went far beyond mere lust?

Why?

Because she didn't trust him.

Like a douse of cold water, the memory of sixty thousand dollars in jewels washed through her brain and sent goose bumps racing over her skin.

She pulled back, gasping, her lips stinging with the force of his kisses.

Elan's eyes slitted open, dark with passion. His full lips parted, moist, as he looked at her.

"I can't." Her words rang clear, decisive, in the deafening silence.

His heavy-lidded stare seared into her. A smile tugged at the corner of his mouth, then he wrapped his hand around her waist and pulled her to him.

"No!" she rasped, stiffening and pulling back. "I won't be the latest addition to your stable. I won't be your new mare."

The slight lift of his lip deepened into an arrogant grin that only intensified her fury. "Every stallion needs a fine mare." His dark words, accompanied by a humorous twinkle of his eyes, challenged her resistance.

"Every stallion has a *herd* of mares. I won't live like that. I already told you, that's how my father treated my mother. I'd rather starve."

By the time she'd finished speaking she'd sprung off the chaise, at the cost of pain shooting through her injured ankle. She stood on the floor, in her bra and borrowed shorts, glaring at him.

His brow furrowed. "What are you talking about? I have no intention of admitting other women to my life. You of all people should know I was fed up with women until you came along."

She lifted her chin and narrowed her eyes. "Mrs. Dixon told

me about the jewelry you ordered. To be delivered to an address in Las Vegas. I think we all know what goes on in Sin City."

Heat flooded her face. Spoken aloud, the gossip—secretarial chitchat about his personal business—cheapened her.

Elan burst out in a laugh. "Mrs. Dixon told you about that? Well, that does surprise me. She seemed the soul of discretion. I'd thought I could trust her with my secrets."

His casual dismissal of her concern made rage streak through her, white-hot.

"How can you laugh it off? How do you think I feel that you're promising me a lifetime commitment when just a few days ago you bought jewelry for another woman?"

Elan laughed again. His throaty chuckle shook his broad chest. "Oh, my, she's jealous as a she-cat! Any minute now I shall have scratch marks on my chest. Sara, you are truly the most wonderful woman alive."

"And you are a...a...." She struggled for words. "A swine!"

Elan laughed again—with delight!—and rubbed a hand over his face, then pushed his fingers back into his tousled hair. His face creased into a broad grin.

The nerve of him! Any minute now she was going to lose her cool and smack him one.

Elan seemed to notice the imminent loss of her last marble, and his expression became more serious. "I ordered those gems for *you*."

Ice crystals formed in her blood as his words seeped into her consciousness.

He's lying.

"I don't believe you. I don't live in Las Vegas."

"No." He hesitated. "But the planner I hired to coordinate the details of our wedding does. She wished to see the gems so she could choose a dress to complement them. I see my subterfuge has undone me."

Sara's brain couldn't seem to process this information. "Our wedding?" She blinked rapidly.

Elan tilted his head and looked sheepish for a moment. "Sara, wait here."

He strode out of the room. Her ankle throbbed and she hopped over to the chaise and sat back down. He'd gone ahead and planned their wedding even though she'd said no?

She should be furious about that. His arrogance had no limit! So why did the idea of him scheming to buy her treasures and dresses and make her his wife cause her whole body to tingle with excitement in a very alarming way?

He returned with his hands behind his back and laughter in his eyes. "Sara, I would like to present you with a small gift that has obviously been the source of some confusion. It was couriered back to me from Las Vegas this morning along with some other items for our wedding."

He held out his hands. Splayed over his broad palms and long fingers, a tangle of gems glittered in the bright sunlight streaming through the skylight. He plucked at one and lifted it between finger and thumb. A string of diamonds linked by a filigree of metal strands. "May I place it around your neck?"

She swallowed. He'd obviously gone to a lot of trouble. "Um, okay."

He sat opposite her, and his musky warmth calmed her as he raised his powerful arms and placed the necklace around her neck. Her skin prickled with awareness as his forearms brushed her shoulders.

He leaned back to survey the result and a smile crept across his lips. "The beauty of this fine design is greatly enhanced by the loveliness of the woman wearing it. Let me get a mirror."

He returned a moment later with a black-rimmed shaving mirror and held it up to her.

"Oh, my goodness." Slim strands of a pale metal—platinum?—danced between brilliant-cut diamonds, weaving back and forth in an intricate pattern that seemed both modern and timeless. The sparkling gems brightened the tones of her skin and picked up the light in her eyes.

"Allow me to fasten the bracelet."

She held out her wrist and was impressed by how easily his large fingers managed the tiny clasp. "I didn't buy earrings as I've noticed you don't wear them. Your lovely ears need no ornamentation." He leaned in and sucked her earlobe in a bold hot swipe that made her catch her breath.

"I…I…don't know what to say." Her hand flew to the jewels at her neck.

Sixty thousand dollars worth of gems.

For her.

"They're a simple token of my affection. A brilliant and beautiful woman such as yourself deserves gifts far more impressive and meaningful than a few sparkly trinkets."

I do?

He took her hand, which trembled in his warm grasp. Her body responded instantly to his touch, heating and straining toward him, nipples tight, fingers and toes tingling.

He touched her chin and lifted it until her gaze met his. "You are my Sara."

"I think I am." She sounded as surprised as she felt. A rush of unexpected tears pricked at her throat and made her bite her lip harder.

He stepped forward, fingers cupped around her jaw. Their mouths came together with magnetic force as his lips closed over hers.

Her head tipped back as she wound her arms around his neck, hugged him to her. She welcomed his tongue, tunneled her fingers into his thick hair and dug them into the hard muscle of his shoulders.

Her breasts, heavy and stirring, craved his touch. He obeyed their call, lifting her bra swiftly over her head before cupping them in his broad palms. Her nipples hummed with pleasure as callused fingers rubbed them delicately to the point of maddening arousal.

She moaned as his tongue grazed her teeth and danced over the tender skin behind her lips. He licked the outside of her lips, then kissed her chin, before diving to lay a trail of kisses along her belly.

They both let out a soft groan as he whisked off her shorts and his mouth penetrated the pale hair at the apex of her thighs. His tongue flicked over her and she jumped, neurons firing as he lit the fuse to what promised to be an awesome fireworks display.

Burying his face between her legs, he licked and sucked, milking her juices with his mouth. Sara's breasts and belly quivered as he drove her to new heights of sensation. Her fingers grasped at his hair and scratched him as she rocked under his fierce caress.

And then the fireworks went off, a whirling Catherine wheel whipped her into a frenzy, seizing her limbs as she braced against the intense sensation. An array of sparklers rained down as her skin sizzled with the heat of passion. Every inch of her felt alive with joy, with sweet wonder at the thrill of making love to Elan.

The weeks of longing, of holding herself back, blew away like distant memories as she gave herself over to the man she loved. With her whole soul she yearned to join with him, to share everything with him, every aspect of her life, herself, her love.

The final barrage of rockets shot through her and left her gasping, breathless, shaken and throbbing in ecstatic release. As she lay in Elan's arms, a sense of peace claimed her, along with the man who had laid siege to her heart and won it.

He trailed a hand over her belly as he raised himself up to bury his face in her neck. Sara wrapped her arms around him and rested her head on his chest. She couldn't imagine being anywhere other than right here, with this man.

He eased up onto the chaise with her and showered her hair and face with tender kisses as their bodies mingled intimately. Resting his head next to hers he snuggled against her and settled a hand on her waist.

His big hand seemed to claim her, and their child.

"We're good together, you and I." He looked at her steadily. His dark eyes shone with wonder she felt, too.

Tentatively, she placed her hand on top of his, then he slid his hand over hers and wrapped his fingers around it.

"We make a good partnership in business," his voice was rough yet soft, like velvet. "And in the bedroom."

"We're not in the bedroom."

Elan nuzzled her and chuckled deep into her ear. "Ah, Sara, you're a breath of life to me. And you're right. I don't think we've ever entered a bedroom together. But that can be rectified immediately."

He slid his powerful arms under her and swept her off the chaise. For once she had no desire to kick and wriggle from his grasp as he carried her down the cool, tiled hallway toward a pair of double oak doors.

"The bedchamber awaits, my lady."

"Thank you, my lord," she mugged.

Elan eased a door open with his elbow and Sara gasped at the sight of the most beautiful bedroom she had ever seen. Everything was white: the smooth travertine-tiled floor, chalky plastered walls, and a giant four-poster bed with gauzy curtains that billowed gently in a mysterious breeze.

A wall of windows spread the desert before them like a giant oil painting, rich in color from the ochre earth to the cloudless indigo sky.

He strode into the oasis of cool whiteness and laid her carefully on snowy satin sheets.

"It's so...white."

"We can change it to whatever you want. My surroundings matter little to me."

"I love it. I've just never seen anything quite like it."

"It's practical in the heat of summer. In my country we know white stays coolest in the hot sun."

"Do you ever wish you could go back to Oman?"

"Yes." His eyes twinkled. "I'd like to show it to you. You'll like it. From the heat and fierce windstorms of the desert, to the soft beaches and calm seas of the coast, it's a study in contrasts that reminds me of someone." A smile tugged at his lips. "It's beautiful, but this is my home."

And you are my wife. He didn't say the words but his eyes claimed her, sweeping over her, taking in her upturned face, her neck encircled by his lavish gift, her full breasts and soft belly, the unfolded length of her legs, before fixing her again with his purposeful stare. Sara suppressed a shudder at the strange feeling of being taken by force—with a mere glance.

Her reaction to Elan overwhelmed her. The connection between them was so powerful, beyond her control, a little frightening. But the maddening undercurrent of constant desire that had threatened their professional partnership now revealed itself as a fire that could fuel the most intense kind of partnership possible.

"Sara," Elan raised her fingers almost to his lips, which parted, poised for a kiss. His eyes lifted to hers, and the intensity of his dark gaze stole her breath. "Will you be my wife?"

Eleven

"Yes."

The only possible answer slipped from her mouth. Every cell in her body breathed it as a massive exhale of relief.

Elan reached into the pocket of his jeans, and retrieved one last piece from the matching set of jewelry.

The ring.

A single diamond in an exquisite setting of smooth pale metal.

She struggled to hold her hand steady as he slid the ring onto her finger. A rush of emotion swept through her as his mouth closed over hers, inhaling her as they seized each other. She gave herself over to him totally, all doubt and fear evaporating in the heat of their kiss. Their baby stirred in her belly, shifting and settling between them as they fell back on the bed to spend the morning in each other's arms.

* * *

Sara shifted restlessly on the leather chaise in the den, flipping idly through a book as the white spotlight of high-noon sun rose to fill the skylight above her.

Elan blew into the room like a desert sirocco, but instead of the work-worn jeans she'd grown used to, he looked devastatingly elegant in a dark suit, white shirt and red-striped tie. His "boss" uniform.

"Are you going into the office?" Sara sat up and put her book aside. "I'll come with you. I'm ready to get back into the swing of things." Three days in the lap of air-conditioned, no-comforts-denied luxury had her a little stir-crazy.

"No need." He smiled. "I've conducted all today's meetings via videoconference from my study."

"Oh."

His smile widened, and excitement shone in his eyes. "And I've made our announcement."

An unexpected rush of fear assaulted her. "You told people at the office we're getting married?"

"And that we're having a child together." He pinned her with a midnight stare that defied her to protest.

"Gosh, it seems so…sudden." The baby shifted, kneeing her in the ribs, and she laid a hand on her belly to calm it.

He lifted his chin. "Don't you wish to share our joy with the world?"

"Yes, but…" But what? "Maybe it would have been nice for us to tell people together."

Elan pursed his lips slightly and nodded. "You're right. From now on we'll be doing many things together. But you need rest. You're recovering from an injury. The less you do right now, the better."

"My leg hardly hurts at all anymore."

"Excellent. And your beautiful posterior?"

She smiled. "I think all those kisses had magical healing powers."

He grinned. "Perhaps tonight we'll apply more 'medicine,' but now I have an appointment to keep. I've applied for the licenses and contacted a justice to perform the ceremony."

"What?" Her stomach clenched as another wave of apprehension rose inside her.

"We must marry right away. You're already my wife in many ways, but I wish you to be my wife in the eyes of the world."

He reached out and took her hand. "It'll be a simple ceremony, just you, me, the justice, and Olga my cook to bear witness. The wedding planner has secured a talented photographer who'll record the event, and take pictures of the bride."

"But I..." Sara was speechless that he'd gone ahead and arranged everything without asking her. She gently pulled her hand out of his grasp and used it to steady herself on the chaise that was starting to feel like a jail bunk.

"What, my sweet?"

"I...I always wanted a big wedding." Tears threatened, stinging her eyes and tugging at the back of her throat. "With all my family there. My brothers and sisters. I always wanted my oldest brother to give me away." She looked up at him. "His name's Derek." She blinked her tears back. "You don't even know the names of my siblings. I want them to meet you."

"There'll be time for that later. I look forward to meeting your family. We'll fly them all here to visit. Perhaps we'll have a big celebration party with them after our baby is born."

She realized she hadn't even phoned her family to tell them she was getting married. Elan had her so thoroughly cosseted in a cocoon of comfort that the outside world—including her own beloved brothers and sisters—seemed a universe away, almost forgotten.

"A skilled seamstress will visit the house tomorrow afternoon to fit you for your dress."

"My dress? The one the planner chose to match the jewels?"

"Exactly."

He laid both hands on her belly, one on either side. The gesture sent a warm shudder of sensation rippling through her. Elan lowered his lips and kissed her belly so tenderly that her heart squeezed with irrational joy.

His cheek rested just above her belly button, his ear pressed to her skin, as if he listened to their child. "I long to give our baby a name. My name."

He lifted his head and looked at her, dark eyes glittering. "And I long for you to bear my name, to be mine forever."

Her heart clenched again, but this time anxiety mingled with her joy. Everything was moving so fast, and she wasn't in control at all. "I left several things unfinished at the office. I really need to go in and sort through some files so I can work effectively from here."

"Sara," Elan chuckled as he rose to his feet. "You'll be my wife, there's no need for you to labor to make a living. You'll want for nothing."

"But I like working, and I have debts to pay off, huge debts." She looked at him cautiously, wondering what his reaction would be.

He waved a dismissive hand in the air. "Your debts are erased."

"What? You paid them?"

He nodded.

"How did you know...?"

"I have my ways." He tapped the side of his nose mysteriously. "As I said, you won't need to think about money from now on. Rest my sweet, so you'll walk with ease at our wedding next week."

He leaned forward and settled a kiss on her cheek. Her blood heated at the mere touch of his lips. As he drew back, her hand flew to the spot where the skin still burned. Her breasts stirred and her nipples lifted, as she yearned—as always—for his caress.

She struggled to regain control of her senses. To regain control of her life. "I want to do my job. I want to have a career, I'm ambitious and I've worked hard...."

Elan leaned into her and licked her mouth as she spoke, swiping his tongue across her lips in a way that erased her words and scattered her thoughts like dust in a breeze.

His left hand cupped her breast and his thumb strummed her nipple as his right hand seized her by the back of her neck. He plunged his tongue into her mouth and she gasped as a throb of agonizing pleasure shook her.

His fingers drifted down the curve of her waist to her hip, then jerked hard on her silk shorts and panties, tugging them down as he leaned into her, pushing her back on the chaise.

Her body melted like wax as his fingers penetrated the treacherously moist flesh of her sex. As his tongue probed her mouth, his broad, stiff finger entered her and she gasped with pleasure, her cry lost against his kiss.

She shuddered hard as he took control of her, working her with his fingers and mouth, driving her beyond the bounds of reason into a different realm where she wanted nothing more than to give herself to him totally, holding nothing back.

As she lay quivering and powerless from the force of her release, Elan eased up her shorts, kissed her once more on the lips, and said, "I have legal business in town, my Sara. I'll be back soon."

His smile was one of confident mastery as he gave her one last, lingering look before he turned on his heel and swept out of the room.

My Sara.

The words reverberated in her ears as she lay there, her limbs heavy with sated desire.

Elan was a hurricane that lifted her off her feet and swept her away on a gust of passion. Drained of strength, will, everything but the waves of pure pleasure she floated on, she drifted into a fitful daytime sleep.

* * *

She jolted awake with a gasp, shaking her head to try and dislodge the ugly images of her nightmare. She'd been covered with gold paint, gleaming, sweating in the hot, desert sun.

"How lovely you look," people had murmured as they passed her.

"I can't breathe!" she'd tried to shout. But no words came out. She recognized the image from an article she'd read about the making of the movie *Goldfinger.* When the actress was painted gold for her role, they had to be careful to leave a large area of skin on her stomach unpainted, or else she would suffocate.

"I'm suffocating!" she burst out.

She didn't know how long she'd been asleep. She wasn't even entirely sure what day it was. She thought she'd been here three days, but maybe it was more?

Elan had seized her life and painted it gold. She sprang off the chaise and winced as her injured ankle reminded her of its existence.

But it was almost healed. There was no reason for her to lie around like a pig being fattened for slaughter.

A movie preview of her life flashed through her mind. A pampered existence where all her needs were taken care of, where she wanted for nothing, wanted nothing…except Elan.

The power he had over her frightened her. That he could silence her protests with his mouth, invade her body with pleasure that stole all rational thought. That he could snatch her life from under her, keep her cosseted in a gilded existence, even pay off what she owed—to leave her permanently in his debt.

She couldn't live like that.

Was he back? She stole across the cool tiled floor in her bare feet and opened the door out into the hallway.

"Elan?"

She had to tell him, right now, that her life was her own, that she needed to make her own decisions, pursue her career goals, pave her own path. She couldn't be a whole person, or a good mother to her child, any other way.

"Elan?" He must still be out.

She limped slightly as she hurried along the long hallway. Shafts of light beaming through the skylights told her it must be late afternoon. She hadn't been outside in three whole days.

She opened the back door and stepped outside to drink in the warm desert air. And she saw something that made her breath catch in her throat.

Her bike. Or what was left of it.

She hobbled over to the disconnected, mangled pile of metal: the wheels stripped of their tires, the chain limp, the handlebars upside down so the fork of the bike stuck in the air. Goose bumps crawled over her arms as she noticed the padded covering had been ripped right off the seat. The bike might have been damaged in the accident, but not to this extent. Amid the clutter lay a wrench and a greasy rag.

Her bike had been deliberately pulled apart.

How on earth had her bike made it to his house? Elan was a man who made things happen. Whatever he wanted.

She knew he hated her bike, and now he'd destroyed it. Nuts and bolts littered the sandy ground and the tires wilted in the sun like molted snake skins. The last symbol of her freedom and independence lay in ruins.

"No!"

The protest emerged as a howl of anguish that reverberated in the desert air, rang across the flat plain, bounced off the buildings, and carried toward the distant mountains. But there was no one to hear it.

Where was her family? Her friends? She had only Elan.

He's never said he loves me. He wanted her to be his wife, yes, but as she knew from harsh personal experience that was *not* the same thing.

When he grew tired of her she'd have nothing and no one. She'd be just like her mother, trapped by guilt, obligation, tradition, and without the means to leave.

I've got to get out of here.

Her throat so tight that she gasped for breath, Sara scanned the horizon. Her bike was far beyond repair. She ran back into the house and hunted for a phone.

She asked information for the name of a taxi service, called, and gave them directions to Elan's ranch. She found her backpack, which mercifully still contained her wallet and the now-wrinkled work attire she'd been carrying when she'd had her accident.

The taxi was coming from miles away. Would it get there before Elan returned? She prayed it would. Elan would never willingly let her go and she knew she didn't have the power to stop him. One look from him, not even a single word, and she'd be falling into his arms, all other considerations forgotten.

"She'll bend to my will. It's only a matter of time." His words came back to her, mocking her with her own vulnerability. She was like the horse he sought to subdue on her first visit to his ranch. *I feed her, care for her, give her shelter from the sun. She will learn these things come with a price. And she'll learn to pay it.*

The price is too high.

A tear rolled down her cheek as she removed her ring, and she shivered at the naked sensation she felt without it. She placed it with its glittering companions on the kitchen table and wrote Elan a letter in which she tried to be as honest as possible. He deserved at least that much. She wrote that she hoped some time—in the future—they would establish a means to give him some access to his child. But not yet. First she needed time to get over him.

A lot of time.

The distant hum of a car engine made her dart to the window, clutching her letter.

Thank God, the cab was here. She'd worried about not being able to make the once-a-day train to Chicago if it didn't come fast enough.

She left the letter on the kitchen table despite a stab of regret. She snatched up her backpack, and hurried outside as fast as her sore ankle would let her.

"The train station, please." The train station was only a few hundred yards from her apartment but she didn't dare go there. Elan might find her. Her neighbor Sylvia would be willing to box up her few possessions and forward them to Wisconsin for a couple of hundred dollars. Money well spent if it would buy her freedom back. And she'd pay Elan back every penny he'd put toward her debts, no matter how long it took.

She didn't look behind her as the cab roared away along the straight road. If she did she might weaken at the sight of the lovely house that might have been her home.

Don't think about it. Just go. Run while you can, there'll be time for crying later.

At the station she paced back and forth waiting for the train, ankle throbbing. Her baby was madly active, kicking and rolling, jumping and bumping against her. It must be her nerves, jangled and sizzling with adrenaline that had her and her child in such turmoil.

She wished the train would come before she might weaken.

Don't think about him.

She didn't even want to think his name. But a fragmentary memory would slip unbidden into her mind—the black hairs that dusted the backs of his powerful hands, the small, delicate ears that sat atop his thickly muscled neck, the way he ran his fingers through his thick hair while he was thinking…

No!

At last the train pulled in and she found herself a seat in the final car, her eyes tearless, fists clenched in resolve. She'd make it. She always had.

* * *

"My Sara!" Elan flung open the front door and tossed his jacket on a chair. Preparing all those papers, adding Sara's name to his bank and brokerage accounts, had taken far longer than he expected. He couldn't wait to lose himself in her arms.

He strode along the corridor and gently pushed open the door to the den. He didn't want to awaken her if she was sleeping. The den was empty.

"Sara!" he called along the corridor and his voice echoed back to him off the hard stone.

Where on earth is she?

He hurried to the kitchen. Perhaps she was hungry. But the room was empty, as was the dining room, the living room, his bedroom.... She wasn't anywhere to be found in the entire house.

Could she have been abducted? He had never been vulnerable to kidnappers before, since he'd never had any dependents. But since he'd been blabbing all over town about his upcoming marriage to Sara, perhaps he'd placed her life in jeopardy?

He grabbed the phone off the hook in the kitchen and was about to dial 911 when he saw a folded note lying on the stone table.

Amidst the diamonds he given her.

He dropped the phone and seized the folded paper.

Dear Elan,
I'm afraid I cannot marry you...

The rest of the words were a blur as he scanned them, looking for where she had gone.

I am leaving for Wisconsin today. Please don't follow me.
I'll contact you when I'm ready.

The train. It had to be. The local route ended in Chicago—a short distance from her home state. He knew she couldn't drive with her injured ankle, and a plane was unlikely with her fear of flying.

He grabbed his keys and spun out the door, slammed into his car and roared off across the desert. He realized with a jolt that he had no clear idea where she was headed. He knew her debts were with a bank in Milwaukee, the P.I. who'd uncovered them had told him that much, but he didn't know if she was originally from that city. He didn't even know the names of her relatives.

And he had a sickening premonition that once she was gone he would never get her back.

The train left the station only once a day at 4:30 p.m. The clock on the dash read 4:22. He pushed the accelerator to the floor and dust clouds whirled around the car as he ate up the sandy desert road.

He blew into town going way over the speed limit and hammered his hands on the wheel as he sat for precious seconds at a stop light.

4:29.

4:30.

The light changed and he revved away, tires squealing. He turned onto the road leading to the station only to see the train just beginning to move.

Its progress was excruciatingly slow—slow motion—but it was leaving the station without him.

He followed the paved road past its end onto the sandy dirt that followed the track out into the desert. He sped past the train, driving several hundred yards out into the desert, then skidded to a halt on the sand and leaped out.

And he ran. Pelting alongside the track, he glanced back at the train coming up behind him. He would have one chance. He kept a steady pace, looking back to find the handhold he'd aim for—the long metal handles on either side of the doors.

The rattling sound of metal wheels on the track clamored in his ears as the first car caught up with him. He quickened his pace and as the handle sped past him he grabbed it and swung himself up onto the steps. He tugged the heavy door open with tremendous effort and hurled himself headlong into the moving car.

The force of the motion flung him to his knees on the floor inside and he paused there a moment on all fours, catching his breath as a wave of stinging relief seared him.

Heads craned to look at him as he scrambled to his feet.

Sara? He scanned the seats, looking for her soft, pale hair amongst the few passengers and not seeing it. He wrenched open the connecting door to the car behind, and stepped through.

Striding along the car, he searched faces, and each one that wasn't her pricked him with a sharp needle of anxiety. He shoved into the next car, heart pounding and sweat trickling along his spine as he prowled down the aisle.

Where was she?

The sight of blond hair falling over a down turned face made his heart seize, but a stranger looked up at him—eyes wide with alarm—as he stopped to lean over her.

The third car had one occupant, an elderly male whose eyes tracked Elan as he plowed onward down the aisle. Only one more car. If he'd miscalculated and she wasn't on the train…

But she was.

As he tugged aside the heavy door between the cars he recognized her instantly. She stood at the end of the aisle, her back to him as she gazed out the rear window of the train at the track streaming out behind.

"Sara!"

She wheeled around, startled by his strangled cry of joy. Relief roared through him. He closed the distance between them at a run, and seized her wrist as he reached her.

"Why did you leave me?" The question flew from his mouth.

Her eyes glittered with tears that streamed down her cheeks. The sight of them tore at his heart.

"Don't cry, my Sara. There are no problems we can't solve together." He pressed his lips to her hand as fierce emotion flared in his chest. The prospect of losing Sara had almost deprived him of his senses. "Thank the stars I've found you. We can get off at the next station and take a cab home."

She looked at him, and her forehead wrinkled in perplexity as her eyes blinked back tears.

"I can't."

Her words emerged as a choking sob. Ten seconds earlier she'd clawed at the window, muttering his name under her breath. She wanted to stay, no matter what the cost. She loved him, she needed him more than her independence, more than her pride.

But now, as he gripped her hand, his black eyes bored into her and his mouth issued another command, her only impulse was to resist.

"You can't leave me." Elan's face was contorted with emotion.

"I can," she whispered, her eyes dropping to avoid the raw pain she saw in his. "I must."

"But why?"

"You read my letter?" She struggled to keep her voice audible.

"It said you couldn't marry me, and that you were leaving today…there wasn't time to read the rest." He dropped her wrist and shoved his hands into his pockets, as if hunting for the paper. "I don't have it with me."

A choking sound, half sob, half laugh, escaped Sara's throat. "You didn't even read it!" She shook her head. "You didn't even care what I had to say. You just knew you had to come after me, regardless of what I wanted."

"I… I…" He held out his hands, his gesture pleading with her. "I couldn't let you go."

"That's just it," her voice emerged high-pitched with desperation. "You couldn't *let* me. You know best, in your mind you always know best. You knew you had to marry me, and you didn't quit trying until I said yes.

"Once you had my assent you whipped my life out from under me and replaced it with a new one, without even asking what I wanted. I'm my own person, Elan, whether you like it or not, and I'm not going to become anyone's pampered possession, locked in a golden cage while you fly free."

She paused for breath.

His lips twitched, no doubt with the urge to protest and silence her, but he didn't speak. He held her gaze, silent. The emotion she read in his dark eyes threatened to rock her resolve.

At last he spoke. "I love you, Sara." His words didn't emerge as a demand, or an order. They were soft, an apology, an offering. "I simply love you."

Her heart quivered at his declaration.

He loved her.

Part of her wanted to jump in his arms, but caution held her steady. "I love you too, Elan," she whispered, the words torn from her by the raw agony she read in his stiff posture. "But sometimes even love isn't enough."

She squeezed her eyelids against fresh tears.

"You're my wife, you know you are, we don't need a piece of paper or a fancy gown. Our marriage is written in the stars."

As he said it she could see his hands jerk as he fought to keep from reaching out to her. She ached with the need to touch him, to hold him, to take him in her arms and soothe him—to comfort them both.

He lifted his chin slightly. "If you don't wish to marry me, so be it." His eyes glittered with pain and defiance, then softened. "But live with me, be my companion, share my life. I won't seek to control you, only to love you—and our child."

A fearful trembling shook Sara as every atom vibrated with longing so intense it was literally painful.

I love you.

Her whole being issued the words and she softened as the force of their love filled the rattling, pounding space of the jolting train car.

Could love be enough? And did she dare take the risk to find out?

"You've entered my empty home—my empty heart—and filled them with love." He stood before her, hands spread, palms up, opening himself to her. "Our love is precious, and we've made a child together. Come home with me."

The appeal of his words loosened her limbs and she longed to fall into his arms and literally let him carry her home. But at the same time her brain crackled with warnings that flashed across her consciousness like electronic billboards.

"What happened to my bike? Did you rip it apart?"

"Yes," he admitted.

The alarms in her brain grew louder. "You deliberately destroyed my only means of transportation?"

"It was broken in the accident. And you know I bought you a new car." He shoved a hand through his hair. "To be honest, the accident scared the hell out of me. It made me so afraid to lose you." He paused, breathing, dark eyes fixed on hers. "I took my emotions out on your bike. I shouldn't have done it and I apologize. I'll buy you a new bike."

The contrition in his eyes and the strong emotion on his face tugged at her heart. Was he truly sorry? She steadied herself against the metal wall as the train rattled onward. Drew in a deep breath. "*I'll* buy me a new bike."

"Yes." His eyes brightened. "Or even better, we can buy it together. I won't prevent you from living the life you want. I'll be right with you, by your side."

Could he see her resolve weakening? "What about at the office? I want to work." She held her chin high.

"Absolutely. We'll share the boardroom—" the gleam in his

eyes turned into a sparkle, "as well as the bedroom. We'll raise our child together and build our company together. A true marriage of equals."

Was it possible? Her heart swelled with the answer *yes* and her arms ached to grab him and hug him.

But doubts—fears—still sneaked around the edges of her mind.

"Elan, neither you nor I knows what a happy marriage is. Our parents were miserable—they destroyed each other—how can we escape that legacy?"

Elan stood, feet apart, braced against the rattling of the train. "We'll forge a new legacy, one not based on worn-out patterns that limit us both. Already you've proved you're strong enough to stand beside me, to stand up to me, to shape our lives with a force equal to mine. Let us break the mold."

He held out a broad hand, palm up, the lines where a palmist could read his future raised to her like an offering. Sara studied the dark creases bisecting his palm, the roadmap that held his fate—and hers.

She rocked a little, shifted to keep her footing on the moving train and suddenly her hand was on Elan's as she grabbed him for balance.

His fingers closed around hers, and she shivered at the reassuring sensation of his big hand steadying her, offering her the support she needed. She could almost feel the lines of their hands fuse together—lifeline, head line, heart line—their destinies becoming inseparable.

Something flowed between them—from his eyes to hers, from her hands to his, a flow of love and positive energy that could power them both for a lifetime.

"Come home with *me*," she whispered, filled with sudden resolve. "Come to Wisconsin with me and meet my family. Come on this journey with me and learn who I am."

Surprise widened Elan's eyes and he blinked. His lips parted as emotion washed across his face, softening his hard features. His eyes shone as his hand tightened around hers. "Yes," he said forcefully. "Yes. We'll go on this journey together." A smile quivered across his mouth. "I'll travel with you wherever you wish to go, my Sara."

He squeezed her hand and she felt a big grin spread across her face. They flew together, arms and legs tangling in the rush to close any distance between them. Her lips stung with the force of his kiss as his mouth closed over hers.

Her body melted into his as his tongue filled her mouth. She buried her hands in his shirt, tugging at it as she strained to touch the hot, vivid skin beneath. Her head thrown back, she writhed as Elan sucked at the pulse point on her neck.

Then she gasped as she realized the train was pulling into the next station.

Elan's eyes opened as she pulled away from him. His pupils were dilated and his face glazed with a sheen of lust and perspiration.

"What?"

"The station."

They collapsed in laughter as they fell toward the closest seats.

"I have no ticket," said Elan, his mouth fighting a grin. "I don't even have my wallet."

"Don't worry, I'll take care of you." She looked at him as she reached into her backpack, wondering how he'd take this first assertion of her right to pay her own way—and his.

He'd settled back into his seat with a satisfied smile, hands behind his head, elbows in the air.

"Take care of me, my Sara, and I'll take care of you."

"It will be my pleasure."

Epilogue

Nine months later, Lions Club Hall, Seminee, Wisconsin

"Oh, he looks so sweet in his tiny tux!" Erin chucked the baby's chubby chin. "I can't believe you managed to find one that small."

"Find it? Are you kidding? Elan had it made by his tailor in London. We had to measure little Ben's inside leg. You should have seen him kicking." Sara giggled. "I'm just glad he's outside of me so I can fit into a real wedding dress, not a white satin tent."

"You look lovely." Her sister bit her lip.

"Oh, don't start bawling again!"

"I'm just so happy for you, and for Elan. I can't believe we've only known him a few months. I feel like he's always been part of our family."

"He does, too. And being around us has triggered his dormant family instincts. You've seen him with his brothers over the past

week. It's like…he's not afraid to care about people anymore."
Uh-oh. She was getting choked up now. There was such affection between the three handsome men that it was hard to believe—and so sad—they'd missed so much time together. Things would be different from now on, she'd make sure of it.

"Speaking of his brothers…" Erin fanned herself, sending blond hair and chiffon dress ruffles fluttering. "Hot!"

Sara smiled. "Stay away from Quasar, he's a notorious playboy," she whispered, glancing at the blue-eyed charmer surrounded—as usual—by a circle of blushing girls.

"Will do. I have bad luck with that type," Erin winked. "But what about Salim? He looks so…dignified. Like he needs someone to loosen him up."

"A tall order, I suspect. He inherited the family business and all the responsibilities that come with it at a young age. And Elan says he never got over his college girlfriend."

"Bummer. Maybe I could help him get over her?" Erin raised her eyebrows. "Then again, I'm not sure I want to move all the way to Oman."

"You'd better not! We're counting on you coming down to Nevada. Elan has a grand vision of our entire family gathered around the table for dinner every evening."

"Does he really? He's so sweet. Then I guess he's not going to quit trying to get us all to move down there, is he?"

Sara shook her head. "Nope. Elan doesn't quit until he gets what he wants. I have firsthand experience of that."

"Well, maybe I'd like the desert air. And the job offer is pretty tempting. Do you really think I have what it takes to be an event planner?"

"Definitely." She squeezed her sister's arm. "If I can be VP of Business Development, you can be an event planner. You run your family single-handed—there's no challenge greater than that. And our kids will have a great time together in the new on-site daycare."

Erin narrowed her eyes as she raised them to look behind Sara. "You're as bad as he is."

"She's worse." Elan's voice tickled Sara's ear as he slid his arms around her waist, surprising her from behind. A warm shiver of pleasure rippled though her. "But think how your children will thrive in the healthy climate where they can play outdoors all year long."

"I've heard the sales pitch," Erin winked at him and hoisted Ben up onto her shoulder.

"I hope Ben doesn't spit up on your lovely dress." Sara turned to Elan. "Where's Derek? Does he have the rings?" She was anxious to get started on the ceremony.

"Salim has the rings, my Sara. He's the best man. Your brother will be walking down the aisle with you, remember."

She sucked in a long breath and smiled. "I do have it all straight in my head, really, I'm just so...so..."

"Happy?" Elan had moved in front of her and he lifted an eyebrow as his lips curved into a smile.

"Yes. So happy." She bit her lip. "I just can't wait to be your wife."

"Nor I to be your husband."

He laid a gentle kiss on her cheek and heat bloomed under his lips in a way that never failed to surprise her, though they spent every day together.

He looked at her for a moment, eyes shining, then turned to lift his son from Erin's arms. He smoothed the baby's thick, dark hair off his tiny forehead and settled him against his broad, tuxedo-clad shoulder. "There's no rush. We have the rest of our lives together, and I mean to savor every glorious minute."

He leaned forward until his mouth brushed her ear and

sparked a sizzling response. "Though I confess, I'm anxious to enjoy the pleasures of our wedding night."

Sara felt her body flush inside her virginal white dress as her nipples strained against the delicate satin. "Just keep your hands off me until after the ceremony. You know I'm not that kind of girl."

They all exploded into helpless giggles as little Ben surprised them with the wonderful throaty chuckle of his first laugh.

* * * * *

Every Life Has More
Than One Chapter™

Award-winning author Stevi Mittman delivers another hys-
terical mystery, featuring Teddi Bayer, an irrepressible
heroine, and her to-die-for hero, Detective Drew Scoones.
After all, life on Long Island can be murder!

*Turn the page for a sneak peek
at the warm and funny fourth book,
WHOSE NUMBER IS UP, ANYWAY?,
in the Teddi Bayer series,
by STEVI MITTMAN.
On sale August 7*

CHAPTER 1

"Before redecorating a room, I always advise my clients
to empty it of everything but one chair. Then I suggest they
move that chair from place to place, sitting in it, until the
placement feels right. Trust your instincts when deciding
on furniture placement. Your room should 'feel right.'"

—TipsFromTeddi.com

Gut feelings. You know, that gnawing in the pit of your stomach
that warns you that you are about to do the absolute stupidest thing
you could do? Something that will ruin life as you know it?

I've got one now, standing at the butcher counter in King
Kullen, the grocery store in the same strip mall as L.I. Lanes, the
bowling alley cum billiard parlor I'm in the process of redecorating for its "Grand Opening."

I realize being in the wrong supermarket probably doesn't sound
exactly dire to you, but you aren't the one buying your father a
brisket at a store your mother will somehow know isn't Waldbaum's.

And then, June Bayer isn't your mother.

The woman behind the counter has agreed to go into the
freezer to find a brisket for me, since there aren't any in the case.
There are packages of pork tenderloin, piles of spareribs and rolls
of sausage, but no briskets.

Warning Number Two, right? I should be so out of here.

But no, I'm still in the same spot when she comes back out,

brisketless, her face ashen. She opens her mouth as if she is going to scream, but only a gurgle comes out.

And then she pinballs out from behind the counter, knocking bottles of Peter Luger Steak Sauce to the floor on her way, now hitting the tower of cans at the end of the prepared foods aisle and sending them sprawling, now making her way down the aisle, careening from side to side as she goes.

Finally, from a distance, I hear her shout, "He's deeeeeeaaaad! Joey's deeeeeaaaad."

My first thought is *You should always trust your gut.*

My second thought is that now, somehow, my mother will know I was in King Kullen. For weeks I will have to hear "What did you expect?" as though whenever you go to King Kullen someone turns up dead. And if the detective investigating the case turns out to be Detective Drew Scoones...well, I'll never hear the end of that from her, either.

She still suspects I murdered the guy who was found dead on my doorstep last Halloween just to get Drew back into my life.

Several people head for the butcher's freezer and I position myself to block them. If there's one thing I've learned from finding people dead—and the guy on my doorstep wasn't the first one—it's that the police get very testy when you mess with their murder scenes.

"You can't go in there until the police get here," I say, stationing myself at the end of the butcher's counter and in front of the Employees Only door, acting as if I'm some sort of authority. "You'll contaminate the evidence if it turns out to be murder."

Shouts and chaos. You'd think I'd know better than to throw the word *murder* around. Cell phones are flipping open and tongues are wagging.

I amend my statement quickly. "Which, of course, it probably isn't. Murder, I mean. People die all the time, and it's not always in hospitals or their own beds, or..." I babble when I'm nervous, and the idea of someone dead on the other side of the freezer door makes me very nervous.

So does the idea of seeing Drew Scoones again. Drew and I have this on-again, off-again sort of thing…that I kind of turned off.

Who knew he'd take it so personally when he tried to get serious and I responded by saying we could talk about *us* tomorrow—and then caught a plane to my parents' condo in Boca the next day? In July. In the middle of a job.

For some crazy reason, he took that to mean that I was avoiding him and the subject of *us*.

That was three months ago. I haven't seen him since.

The manager, who identifies himself and points to his nameplate in case I don't believe him, says he has to go into *his cooler.* "Maybe Joey's not dead," he says. "Maybe he can be saved, and you're letting him die in there. Did you ever think of that?"

In fact, I hadn't. But I had thought that the murderer might try to go back in to make sure his tracks were covered, so I say that I will go in and check.

Which means that the manager and I couple up and go in together while everyone pushes against the doorway to peer in, erasing any chance of finding clean prints on that Employee Only door.

I expect to find carcasses of dead animals hanging from hooks, and maybe Joey hanging from one, too. I think it's going to be very creepy and I steel myself, only to find a rather benign series of shelves with large slabs of meat laid out carefully on them, along with boxes and boxes marked simply Chicken.

Nothing scary here, unless you count the body of a middle-aged man with graying hair sprawled faceup on the floor. His eyes are wide open and unblinking. His shirt is stiff. His pants are stiff. His body is stiff. And his expression, you should forgive the pun—is frozen. Bill-the-manager crosses himself and stands mute while I pronounce the guy dead in a sort of *happy now?* tone.

"We should not be in here," I say, and he nods his head emphatically and helps me push people out of the doorway just in time to hear the police sirens and see the cop cars pull up outside the big store windows.

Bobbie Lyons, my partner in Teddi Bayer Interior Designs (and also my neighbor, my best friend and my private fashion police), and Mark, our carpenter (and my dogsitter, confidant, and ego booster), rush in from next door. They beat the cops by a half step and shout out my name. People point in my direction.

After all the publicity that followed the unfortunate incident during which I shot my ex-husband, Rio Gallo, and then the subsequent murder of my first client—which I solved, I might add— it seems like the whole world, or at least all of Long Island, knows who I am.

Mark asks if I'm all right. (Did I remember to mention that the man is drop-dead-gorgeous-but-a-decade-too-young-for-me- yet-too-old-for-my-daughter-thank-god?) I don't get a chance to answer him because the police are quickly closing in on the store manager and me.

"The woman—" I begin telling the police. Then I have to pause for the manager to fill in her name, which he does: *Fran*.

I continue. "Right. Fran. Fran went into the freezer to get a brisket. A moment later she came out and screamed that Joey was dead. So I'd say she was the one who discovered the body."

"And you are…?" the cop asks me. It comes out a bit like who do I *think* I am, rather than who am I really?

"An innocent bystander," Bobbie, hair perfect, makeup just right, says, carefully placing her body between the cop and me.

"And she was just leaving," Mark adds. They each take one of my arms.

Fran comes into the inner circle surrounding the cops. In case it isn't obvious from the hairnet and bloodstained white apron with Fran embroidered on it, I explain that she was the butcher who was going for the brisket. Mark and Bobbie take that as a signal that I've done my job and they can now get me out of there. They twist around, with me in the middle, as if we're a Rockettes line, until we are facing away from the butcher counter. They've managed to propel me a few steps toward the exit when disaster—in the form of a Mazda RX7 pulling up at the loading curb—strikes.

Mark's grip on my arm tightens like a vise. "Too late," he says.

Bobbie's expletive is unprintable. "Maybe there's a back door," she suggests, but Mark is right. It's too late.

I've laid my eyes on Detective Scoones. And while my gut is trying to warn me that my heart shouldn't go there, regions farther south are melting at just the sight of him.

"Walk," Bobbie orders me.

And I try to. Really.

Walk, I tell my feet. *Just put one foot in front of the other.*

I can do this because I know, in my heart of hearts, that if Drew Scoones was still interested in me, he'd have gotten in touch with me after I returned from Boca. And he didn't.

Since he's a detective, Drew doesn't have to wear one of those dark blue Nassau County Police uniforms. Instead, he's got on jeans, a tight-fitting T-shirt and a tweedy sports jacket. If you think that sounds good, you should see him. Chiseled features, cleft chin, brown hair that's naturally a little sandy in the front, a smile that…well, that doesn't matter. He isn't smiling now.

He walks up to me, tucks his sunglasses into his breast pocket and looks me over from head to toe.

"Well, if it isn't Miss Cut and Run," he says. "Aren't you supposed to be somewhere in Florida or something?" He looks at Mark accusingly, as if he was covering for me when he told Drew I was gone.

"Detective Scoones?" one of the uniforms says. "The stiff's

in the cooler and the woman who found him is over there." He jerks his head in Fran's direction.

Drew continues to stare at me.

You know how when you were young, your mother always told you to wear clean underwear in case you were in an accident? And how, a little farther on, she told you not to go out in hair rollers because you never knew who you might see—or who might see you? And how now your best friend says she wouldn't be caught dead without makeup and suggests you shouldn't, either?

Okay, today, *finally,* in my overalls and Converse sneakers, I get it.

I brush my hair out of my eyes. "Well, I'm back," I say. As if he hasn't known my exact whereabouts. The man is a detective, for heaven's sake. "Been back awhile."

Bobbie has watched the exchange and apparently decided she's given Drew all the time he deserves. "And we've got work to do, so…" she says, grabbing my arm and giving Drew a little two-fingered wave goodbye.

As I back up a foot or two, the store manager sees his chance and places himself in front of Drew, trying to get his attention. Maybe what makes Drew such a good detective is his ability to focus.

Only what he's focusing on is me.

"Phone broken? Carrier pigeon died?" he asks me, taking in Fran, the manager, the meat counter and that Employees Only door, all without taking his eyes off me.

Mark tries to break the spell. "We've got work to do there, you've got work to do here, Scoones," Mark says to him, gesturing toward next door. "So it's back to the alley for us."

Drew's lip twitches. "You working the alley now?" he says.

"If you'd like to follow me," Bill-the-manager, clearly exasperated, says to Drew—who doesn't respond. It's as if waiting for my answer is all he has to do.

So, fine. "You knew I was back," I say.

The man has known my whereabouts every hour of the day for as long as I've known him. And my mother's not the only one who won't buy that he "just happened" to answer this particular call. In fact, I'm willing to bet my children's lunch money that he's taken every call within ten miles of my home since the day I got back.

And now he's gotten lucky.

"*You* could have called *me*," I say.

"You're the one who said *tomorrow* for our talk and then flew the coop, chickie," he says. "I figured the ball was in your court."

"Detective?" the uniform says. "There's something you ought to see in here."

Drew gives me a look that amounts to *in or out?*

He could be talking about the investigation, or about our relationship.

Bobbie tries to steer me away. Mark's fists are balled. Drew waits me out, knowing I won't be able to resist what might be a murder investigation.

Finally he turns and heads for the cooler.

And, like a puppy dog, I follow.

Bobbie grabs the back of my shirt and pulls me to a halt.

"I'm just going to show him something," I say, yanking away.

"Yeah," Bobbie says, pointedly looking at the buttons on my blouse. The two at breast level have popped. "That's what I'm afraid of."

HARLEQUIN®

Mediterranean
NIGHTS™

Glamour, elegance, mystery and revenge
aboard the high seas...

Coming in August 2007...

THE TYCOON'S SON

by
award-winning author
Cindy Kirk

Businessman Theo Catomeris's long-estranged
father is determined to reconnect with his son, so
he hires Trish Melrose to persuade Theo to renew
his contract with Liberty Line. Sailing aboard the
luxurious *Alexandra's Dream* is a rare opportunity for
the single mom to mix business and pleasure. But
an undeniable attraction between Trish and Theo is
distracting her from the task at hand....

HM38962

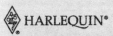

HARLEQUIN®

Super Romance®

*Looking for a romantic, emotional
and unforgettable escape?*

*You'll find it this month and every month
with a Harlequin Superromance!*

Rory Gorenzi has a sense of humor and a sense of
honor. She also happens to be good with children.

Seamus Lee, widower and father of four, needs
someone with exactly those traits.

They meet at the Colorado mountain school owned
by Rory's father, where she teaches skiing and
avalanche safety. But Seamus—and his children—
learn more from her than that....

Look for

GOOD WITH CHILDREN

by Margot Early,

*available August 2007, and these other
fantastic titles from Harlequin Superromance.*

REQUEST YOUR FREE BOOKS!

2 FREE NOVELS PLUS 2 FREE GIFTS!

Passionate, Powerful, Provocative!

YES! Please send me 2 FREE Silhouette Desire® novels and my 2 FREE gifts. After receiving them, if I don't wish to receive any more books, I can return the shipping statement marked "cancel." If I don't cancel, I will receive 6 brand-new novels every month and be billed just $3.80 per book in the U.S., or $4.47 per book in Canada, plus 25¢ shipping and handling per book and applicable taxes, if any*. That's a savings of almost 15% off the cover price! I understand that accepting the 2 free books and gifts places me under no obligation to buy anything. I can always return a shipment and cancel at any time. Even if I never buy another book from Silhouette, the two free books and gifts are mine to keep forever.

225 SDN EEXJ 326 SDN EEXU

Name	(PLEASE PRINT)	
Address		Apt.
City	State/Prov.	Zip/Postal Code

Signature (if under 18, a parent or guardian must sign)

Mail to the **Silhouette Reader Service™:**
IN U.S.A.: P.O. Box 1867, Buffalo, NY 14240-1867
IN CANADA: P.O. Box 609, Fort Erie, Ontario L2A 5X3

Not valid to current Silhouette Desire subscribers.

Want to try two free books from another line?
Call 1-800-873-8635 or visit www.morefreebooks.com.

* Terms and prices subject to change without notice. NY residents add applicable sales tax. Canadian residents will be charged applicable provincial taxes and GST. This offer is limited to one order per household. All orders subject to approval. Credit or debit balances in a customer's account(s) may be offset by any other outstanding balance owed by or to the customer. Please allow 4 to 6 weeks for delivery.

Your Privacy: Silhouette is committed to protecting your privacy. Our Privacy Policy is available online at www.eHarlequin.com or upon request from the Reader Service. From time to time we make our lists of customers available to reputable firms who may have a product or service of interest to you. If you would prefer we not share your name and address, please check here. ☐

SDES07

REASONS FOR REVENGE

A brand-new provocative miniseries by *USA TODAY* bestselling author **Maureen Child** begins with

SCORNED BY THE BOSS

Jefferson Lyon is a man used to having his own way. He runs his shipping empire from California, and his admin Caitlyn Monroe runs the rest of his world. When Caitlin decides she's had enough and needs new scenery, Jefferson devises a plan to get her back. Jefferson *never* loses, but little does he know that he's in a competition....

Don't miss any of the other titles from the REASONS FOR REVENGE trilogy by *USA TODAY* bestselling author **Maureen Child**.

SCORNED BY THE BOSS #1816
Available August 2007

SEDUCED BY THE RICH MAN #1820
Available September 2007

CAPTURED BY THE BILLIONAIRE #1826
Available October 2007

Only from Silhouette Desire!

COMING NEXT MONTH

**#1813 SEDUCED BY THE WEALTHY PLAYBOY—
Sara Orwig**
The Garrisons
She needed his help to rescue her sinking business…but didn't know his price would be the ultimate seduction.

#1814 THE TEXAN'S SECRET PAST—Peggy Moreland
A Piece of Texas
Starting an affair with his lady partner could have its perks, or it may reveal a truth best left hidden.

#1815 IN BED WITH THE DEVIL—Susan Mallery
Millionaire of the Month
She'd been the mousy girl he'd never looked at twice. Now she was the only woman he wanted in his bed.

#1816 SCORNED BY THE BOSS—Maureen Child
Reasons for Revenge
This millionaire thinks he can win his assistant back with seduction. Then she discovers his ploy and shows him two can play his game!

**#1817 THE PLAYBOY'S PASSIONATE PURSUIT—
Emilie Rose**
Monte Carlo Affairs
He would stop at nothing to get her between his sheets… The race is on.

**#1818 THE EXECUTIVE'S VENGEFUL SEDUCTION—
Maxine Sullivan**
Australian Millionaires
Five years of secrets and lies have built a wall between them. Is the time finally right for a passionate resolution?

SDCNM0707